windstorm of bliss

A PARANORMAL FANTASY ROMANCE

THE ELEMENTALS MAGIC
BOOK 1

NIKKI RIKER

Nikki Riker

Copyright © 2022 by Nikki Riker

All rights reserved.

No part of this publication may be reproduced, distributed or transmitted in any form or by any means, without prior written permission.

This is a work of fiction. Names, characters, places, and incidents are a product of the author's imagination. Locales and public names are sometimes used for atmospheric purposes. Any resemblance to actual people, living or dead, or to businesses, companies, events, institutions, or locales is completely coincidental.

author's note

Hey reader! I'm so glad you decided to grab my book. I do hope you enjoy the story and characters within. Oh, be sure to join my mailing list to stay up-to-date with new releases and more.

Click or visit the link below.
NIKKIRIKER.COM

Okay, let's get this story started, shall we?

Happy reading,
Nikki Riker

one

Alma felt the changes in her body for months by the time the phone call from her grandmother came, inviting her to visit. The twinges, the shifts in her perception, weren't as alarming as they might have been had she not expected them.

They mirrored the changes she'd gone through at various points in her youth. Once she'd begun showing promising abilities at six, her grandmother kept her every summer from that point on. Alma's bond with her grandmother was strong.

Receiving training from the older woman and pushing her way through adolescence while maintaining as level a mind as she could, became more difficult as the manifestations of her abilities became more prominent.

The phone call and the invitation weren't a friendly request for a visit. Alma knew why her grandmother was inviting her to spend a few weeks at the family home. She wasn't crazy about the interruption of her routine, but she knew she had to obey. An invitation from the family matriarch meant a great deal—particularly in light of

Alma's approaching birthday. If she tried to make an excuse, she would be on the receiving end of increasing pressure from her aunts, uncles, cousins—even her own mother. It wouldn't stop until she agreed. It was easier to give in right away. So Alma put her life on hold and made the seven-hour trek to the small, middle-of-nowhere town, where her grandmother lived. Whatever her grandmother had to talk to her about, it would be important and likely concern her coming of age.

Even at twenty-two, Alma was still considered by certain members of her family to be a child. Not because they were older than her exactly, but because of her still-undeveloped abilities. She had been three when her grandmother first explained to her mother that Alma inherited the traits of the elemental, and with that came certain responsibilities and requirements. Alma's mother had initially been in denial. None of Alma's older siblings had shown signs and her mother had been hopeful the trait would skip the entire generation. By age five, however, her mother couldn't ignore that Alma wasn't simply intelligent. When Alma's ability with language first emerged, it was a spectacle her mother would never forget.

It happened waiting in line at a grocery store. The couple in front argued about something in Japanese, and even though Alma had never heard Japanese in her life she understood every word they were exchanging. Being as young as she was, she didn't understand why the adults were fussing about five cents. So, instinctively, she spoke to them, getting their attention and handed them five cents. The two looked at her, shocked. The look of surprise on her mother's face made Alma wonder what she had done wrong. She hadn't realized her comments had been made in a foreign language. The words had come so readily that she had never considered the possibility what she was doing was strange.

"I'm sorry, Mommy," Alma had said to her mother. She began to tear up thinking about her mother being angry with her. "I didn't mean to talk out of turn, but they were arguing."

Her mother shushed her, and the Japanese couple quickly finished their transaction and left.

From that point forward, there was no way her mother could deny Alma was an elemental—there was no other way to explain the sudden ability she had with languages. She had tested Alma when they arrived home, flipping through the foreign language channels and asking her what the people were saying. Alma only required a few minutes of listening to each to translate. That night, while Alma was in bed, her mother called her grandmother and took her to stay with her that summer. She would need her grandmother's training.

Every summer after, Alma stayed with her grandmother, and gradually learned everything she could about the world she belonged to. She had been taught to control her abilities, to use them to her advantage. Her grandmother had been slightly bewildered by the fact that Alma's traits seemed aligned with air, like her grandfather's had been. Alma's grandmother was a water-aligned elemental and her children mostly had water traits with a few having earth traits. When Alma was nine, her grandfather passed away, leaving the two to figure out her training on their own. Her grandfather had been the one person in the family who knew what elemental air abilities were like.

Alma knew she could expect to come into the full power of her elemental abilities when she was twenty-three. The magic inherent in the abilities was keyed to her birthdate. Since she had been born during the sixth month, she developed abilities in her sixth year. Being born on the 23rd day meant at twenty-three, she would reach her peak.

Because of this, Alma wasn't surprised to get the invitation to visit her grandmother before her birthday. In some respects, she'd been expecting the invitation, knowing there would be details her grandmother would want to convey to her before she came into the full scope of her abilities. She also knew political issues brewed in the elemental world.

When she started visiting her grandmother to receive training and education, it was Alma's introduction to the world of elementals. While they were human, elementals occupied an odd space in the world. Inherent magic courses through their bodies, and that magical energy can be used in a variety of ways. There has never been a way to effectively gauge how a child born into an elemental family would align until they manifested their abilities, if they were born with any. Most elementals gave birth to a similarly aligned child. Only in the last several generations had elemental families of the world intermarried, encouraging more diversity in their offspring. Some of the elementals even married "normal" humans with less than predictable results.

Over the years Alma made contacts among the different families, sitting through boring luncheons with her grandmother. In later years, meeting up with young elementals of her own age for nights of drinking and partying. She hadn't remained close to most of those she met, but Alma had done as she was told and formed acquaintances she maintained minimal contact with. She was marginally aware that her grandmother was one of the ruling elites, potentially the most powerful water-aligned elemental among the living. She was also aware that her grandmother had high expectations for her.

Alma was exhausted by the time she reached her grandmother's home. Her rental car bumped its way down the long, rough driveway that led from the road to the isolated house. It was late and traffic had been more backed up than she had expected, but as she got closer to the house, Alma's fatigue melted away. The energy surrounding the house drew her in, increasing her vitality. It was an effect she remembered from her earliest experiences of arriving at her grandmother's. Her grandmother once said she'd picked the location of her house based on the energy field and had never regretted it.

Alma drove deep into the woods until the house surrounded by an enormous collection of luscious gardens came into view. It had always had restorative powers to everyone who visited—family, friends, even strangers who found themselves lost. Alma pulled through the gloomy darkness of the driveway with trees arching over, scraping the roof of the car. The clearing in front of the house, where her grandmother's truck sat, was lit by a bright white security lamp, giving everything a silvery sheen. Alma shut off the engine. She smiled to herself as she walked toward the light shining from the bay window of the house. She had expected that, despite the late hour, her grandmother would still be awake.

Alma didn't bother knocking. She called quietly as she entered.

"Grams, I'm here!" The sound of a recliner swiveling on

its base floated through the air. She heard her grandmother stand to greet her. Alma hurried from the front door toward the living room and hugged her grandmother tightly, resting her face against the older woman's shoulder. In spite of how serious she knew the meeting was, it was a relief to be around her. Alma took in a deep breath, feeling her grandmother's dark energy, breathing in the smell of lilacs from her perfumed body powder and soap.

"OOh, Alma. It's great to see you, girl." Her grandmother hugged her with less strength but equal enthusiasm. Alma broke away, gesturing for her grandmother to reseat herself and pulled a chair from the other side of the fireplace to face her grandmother. In spite of advanced age, Alma still recognized the qualities that made her grandmother so beautiful—bright green eyes, highly arched eyebrows that remained dark even as her hair had gone white, and bone structure that gave her a mysterious air even when she smiled. Traits Alma had inherited a few of, though she had also inherited many of her grandfather's more prominent traits, including his dark eye color. Alma's grandmother glared at her for a long moment in silence. Alma knew better than to interrupt the appraisal. She sat quietly, despite the natural nervous energy that made her want to fidget.

"I'm happy that you're here," her grandmother finally said, smiling faintly. "You're getting stronger. I can feel it." She studied Alma a moment more. "I can't tell you everything I need to talk to you about tonight, but I'm glad you came."

Alma chuckled, relaxing against the back of the wooden chair. "Of course I came, and thank you," she replied. She respected her grandmother, but for years their relationship had been less formal. "If I hadn't come, you would've sicked Aunt Suzanne, and my own mother, on me."

Alma's grandmother laughed, her bright green eyes sparkling with mischief.

"What they do on their own is none of my business," she protested, smiling to show she knew very well Alma was right. After a moment she subsided, her face growing more serious. "This is very serious, though, Alma. You're coming into your own in such a short time, and there's a lot going on in our world you need to be aware of."

Alma had maintained some ties with elementals she had befriended during her teen years and while she had been at college, so she knew there was unrest, particularly among the less-established families. But that hadn't impacted her—she was low man on the totem pole as far as her family was concerned. Her grandmother, as the matriarch, was more than equipped to handle the politics.

"I know, I know," Alma said, somewhat dismissively. "The Reubens are frustrated with the lack of respect they're getting from the rest of the community, and the Granger family is involved in a feud with the Fishers."

Her grandmother shook her head. "Alma, I know more people among the elemental elite than you do. There's much more to it than that. There's talk of a judgment day. Some of the younger families are exposing themselves to regular humans in a way that can't be tolerated, and the elder elementals are getting restless. There's talk of wiping out families."

Alma was surprised. She had heard about the elder elemental families—those who persisted through generations, whose status was as firmly founded as an ancient noble line. Those families wanted to take firmer steps against the elementals who endangered everyone else by showing off their abilities. She never dreamed anyone would want to obliterate an entire elemental family. The number of elementals had shrunk over the past hundred years as elementals increasingly moved into regular society. They traditionally held themselves apart, keeping lines pure and maintaining power amongst themselves. The abilities of elemental magic were sometimes very strong, which made them dangerous for untrained, unprepared individuals. They were also terrifying for anyone who didn't understand them—who didn't know they were simply a trait one was born with. Elementals had taken great care that references to them specifically were limited in any information ever published about the occult or the paranormal.

"So, there's a lot of tension. That doesn't necessarily mean anything for me," Alma said.

Her grandmother shook her head again, looking worried as well as sad. She took a deep breath and sighed, looking away from Alma briefly and then making eye contact once more.

"You are the strongest of the elementals in this family aside from me," her grandmother said slowly. "That makes you a target for all the disgruntled families. When you come into your abilities fully, you're going to be as strong as I am, and it will take you some time to get accustomed to the increase in power. It's dangerous. I need to prepare you before you come into your inheritance."

Alma absorbed the news. She knew she was strong; other members of her family who exhibited elemental traits had not developed as rapidly as she had. She had moved beyond the simple exercises her cousins struggled with quickly, mastering her abilities as they emerged. She also knew when her powers developed completely, she would have a great deal more to master. It would be more difficult than ever to maintain secrecy as a member of the community and to retain control.

"Am I really that strong?" Alma stared wide-eyed at her grandmother. She hadn't considered the level of her strength in years, since she had stopped competing with family members because her grandmother had insisted she was showing off.

Alma's grandmother nodded slowly. "There are other things we need to talk about, but right now a cup of tea and a piece of cake is what's needed most. Then you need to get some sleep."

Alma knew there was no arguing with her grandmother, no way to insist she wasn't hungry. She also knew better than to offer to help. Her grandmother stood slowly, folding the recliner back onto itself and shakily getting to her feet and walking slightly unsteadily into the kitchen. Her grandmother could still get around, but advanced age stiffened her joints. Her body was less responsive than it had once been, but it was expected. Alma's grandmother, however, was proud and refused to let anyone help her.

Alma took a seat at the kitchen table, twirling a lock of her long brown hair around her finger, and watching as her grandmother closed her eyes a moment, murmuring something to herself. The older woman touched the kettle on the stove and Alma smiled to herself. She knew the little trick her grandmother performed to ensure by means of magic there was enough water for two cups of tea. She moved around the kitchen, taking mugs from a high shelf in the cabinet, then pulling sealed jars of herbs from a rack and adding them to the bottom of the cup while she waited for the water to boil.

Alma knew whatever her grandmother was putting into the mugs, it would be sleep-inducing, and shortly after the "bedtime snack" she would be more than ready for bed. The subtle manipulations of her grandmother had occasionally frustrated her as a teenager, but as her restlessness had increased, along with her abilities, she had often begged her grandmother for a few sachets of the tea to drink on nights when she particularly needed to sleep.

One of her grandmother's gifts—a result of the way she applied her elemental abilities—was an uncanny knowledge of herb weaving, an ability to know what ingredients to blend into a soup, a tea, or a wound dressing, to get the results she wanted.

Alma was deep in thought as she watched her grandmother slicing pound cake to go with the tea. She had grown up knowing magic existed. She had laughed secretly at her peers as they experimented with Wiccan practices, knowing that kind of magic was an echo of what she was learning and the skills she was developing. She smiled as she remembered the time she terrified a coven mistress, in a display of youthful pride, by calling the wind with a whistle on a clear and stagnant day...all because the coven mistress had insisted she just "didn't have the magic" in her. It had been a victorious moment—being able to display some measure of her ability—but her grandmother had given her hell about it afterward. Alma still remembered the scolding she had received: "What good does it possibly do for you to attract attention to your abilities? Don't you realize you could have gotten yourself killed? That was a damn fool stunt, and you know it." At the time, the reprimand stung.

Alma hadn't even put her abilities to full use. Gradually she noticed the reactions to her more "normal" elemental traits and realized that she was regarded by normal humans as something of a freak and that a fear of her could lead to danger—not just for her, but for all elementals.

Alma's grandmother brought the tea and cake to the table, and they ate as Alma asked questions about her grandmother's garden between bites to avoid sitting in silence. The tea was slightly minty with honey-rich floral tones mingled in the warm brew. While Alma didn't know what was in it, she savored it slowly, with bites of the moist cake. By the time she finished her tea and cake, she was sleepy and barely had enough energy to get her suitcase out of the car. Her grandmother preferred to sleep in the recliner, so Alma wished her a good night as she passed the front living room on her way to her bedroom at the back of the house.

She changed into a nightgown and crawled between the crisp, fresh-smelling linens on the bed. She fell asleep almost the moment her head hit the pillow.

two

Alma awoke the next morning feeling changes in her body stronger than ever. She knew the energy from the land around her grandmother's home was partly the cause, but it was also a result of the culmination of her abilities emerging. Her limbs tingled, her mind buzzed. She took a deep breath and waited for the moment to pass, for the sensations to ease away. She had felt them increasing as her body prepared itself.

Her mind focused as she became awake. The wind howled outside the window like the onslaught of a rainstorm, shaking the trees and sending eerie shivers through the bushes. Alma inhaled deeply and the wind calmed, humming a quieter tune.

Part of Alma's training had been to learn the ways her elemental alignment manifested itself as well as the qualities common in the elemental types—water, earth, air, fire. Her grandmother, as a water-aligned elemental, had a talent for gardening, an extreme affinity for growing things. She also had the ability to heal others. Her nature was fluid like the water, almost perverse and with intense emotions and heady resentments. Along with those intense emotions, she had a profound intuition. There had been nothing Alma could keep secret from her grandmother. Even when her mother hadn't caught her, her grandmother called when Alma had done wrong to chastise her privately. And when she was hurting, the compassion her grandmother offered had been a soothing balm for Alma's nervy nature.

Alma, however, had aligned with the air. She'd always had a boundless supply of energy. Where her grandmother was quiet and almost passive, Alma had been boisterous and active, her mind leaping from subject to subject. She came to understand her inability to stay still resulted from the magic coursing through her. Just as the wind can create an infinite supply of energy, it seemed Alma could too. It was as much a part of her as her ability to understand any language. An ability she had put to good use, studying linguistics in college and becoming a freelance translator. Although every language in existence was easily interpreted, she'd always been careful to hedge the number of languages she could translate.

Her high energy was used through an instructor teaching her archery and fencing (and at least slightly ladylike) pursuits for her abilities. As she had come into adolescence, elemental qualities became increasingly more intense, Alma's restless nature transformed into anxiety. An intervention on her grandmother's behalf was needed to help her balance the overwhelming stress before it got too far out of hand. Alma knew she would never be free of the mentally taxing pressures of her abilities, her grandmother's healing powers had given her relief on more than one occasion.

As she had gained command of the more "normal"

traits associated with her elemental alignment, Alma's grandmother had also helped her cultivate more magical parts. She had flown for the first time—on accident—at the age of twelve. Only for a few moments but falling from a tree inspired her—in a panic—to lift herself before she hit the ground. She had taken the scolding for disobeying rules in good stead, particularly since her grandmother had told her not to climb the tree to begin with. When it was done, however, her grandmother fought back a smile and told her wryly she might as well learn to fly on command if she was going to do it.

Alma practiced that entire summer, slowly raising herself up off the ground until she reached the top limbs of the tree she had fallen from. Flight was not an easy trick to manage, but it was one of Alma's favorite talents. As an air elemental, she also communicated and controlled creatures of the air with relative ease. As a teenager, she lured bees to her grandmother's house to pollinate the flowers, and learned the calls of birds, becoming friends with robins, threshers, mockingbirds and more. She had stayed up late one night, communicating with owls that haunted the darkened boughs of a nearby tree until she finally understood them. While she did not have her grandmother's level of psychic intuition, Alma had excelled from an early age in divination, reading tarot or playing cards to get an understanding of the future. She also studied the use of other tools of the trade, including a crystal ball given to her at fifteen by an aunt.

Alma had no real notion of what the final manifestations of her abilities would be. She knew her grandmother, as a young woman, had been formidable. The prediction her grandmother had made the night before, that Alma would be as powerful, was both thrilling and nerve wracking. She couldn't imagine what she would do with the level of power her grandmother possessed with such grace and subtlety. Her grandmother had hinted once that, while Alma was air-aligned, her distinct weather-related talents came from the family's history of water elementals. The rainstorms she summoned—sometimes unconsciously—was one manifestation of that trait, and Alma was uncertain if she wanted that part of her talents strengthened. She told herself firmly repeatedly that whatever gifts she received in the final transformation into a full elemental, she would learn to use them as effectively as the ones she had first developed as a child.

Alma rolled out of bed. It was nearly impossible to linger being as restless as she was. Even though the crackling, electric tingles running up and down her limbs didn't subside once she was up and moving around. The smell of coffee and a lavish breakfast floated on the air to Alma's room. Her grandmother likely knew she was already awake, and her grandmother wouldn't remain patient for long. Alma didn't bother to change out of her nightgown, she brushed her hair and washed her face in the bathroom before walking to the kitchen.

Her grandmother was seated at the table waiting, a cup of coffee in her hand and a feast of a breakfast laid out: scrambled eggs remaining warm in a cast iron skillet, a platter of sausage, freshly made biscuits with a crock of butter and a jar of homemade fig preserves, and yellow grits swimming with butter. It was a breakfast Alma had eaten hundreds of times, and still the comfort of the routine was undeniable.

The only short period in Alma's life when she had been scrawny came between the ages of twelve and thirteen during a growth spurt. That growth spurt left her lanky, which made her self-conscious enough to avoid the boys she'd been attracted to in middle school. Her grandmother had explained to her time and again—her words falling on deaf ears—that as her magical nature asserted itself over the human realities of her genetics, she would become more womanlike. At age fourteen, she filled out. Her curves intensified. By the time she left for college, she had "blossomed" into a woman with a true hourglass figure. She was the envy of many dorm mates and the desire of voracious frat boys. The years of martial arts training came in handy a time or two. Alma had never slept with any of them against her will.

"You must have been having interesting dreams," Alma's grandmother stated calmly, sipping her coffee. Alma sat down and doctored her coffee, adding two spoons of sugar and a healthy dollop of cream from the pitcher her grandmother had placed by her mug.

Alma smiled wryly. "It's been getting more difficult to control the wind while I sleep," Alma admitted, taking a sip of her coffee, and savoring it before she considered the feast in front of her. She felt the intent green eyes watching her and fought down the urge to squirm.

"I don't think controlling the wind is the problem; I think it's controlling yourself." It was a familiar refrain. Alma knew she was right—but it was still maddening to be called out for her lack of self-control. She'd been trying to develop the self-control and self-discipline her grandmother demanded her entire life. So far, the only thing she'd truly learned to manage was her temper. She possessed the negative qualities associated with the air and the positive ones. Wind could often be chaotic and out of control. While she had a genius intellect, her ability to focus on a single task long enough to master it was largely determined by how interested she was. Studying had never been a strong suit for her, nor had organization.

"I'm trying, Grams, but it's a little more difficult to control yourself in your sleep."

Her grandmother smiled slightly, silently acknowledging the truth of Alma's point. According to family lore, as a young woman her grandmother had such intense dreams she once flooded her entire house. Alma thought she could certainly understand her inability to have complete control over the way her dreams disrupted the local wind patterns.

"You'll have to learn. I certainly wouldn't want you to become a nomad once you come into your powers, constantly homeless because of random windstorms and tornadoes."

Alma grinned at the image as she scooped breakfast onto her plate. She had noticed her metabolism getting faster and faster as she approached her transformation. She needed constant high-calorie meals and more than one of her friends had remarked she must have a hollow leg to put away so much food while keeping her voluptuous curves.

"Not like anyone would notice the difference, my apartment always looks like a disaster area anyway." Alma's grandmother let out a rusty chuckle, serving herself in quick movements when Alma had filled her plate. For a moment they ate in silence, Alma savoring the familiar flavors as she stoked her metabolic fires, glancing occasionally at her grandmother. She could sense there was a big "talk" in the works, but she wasn't about to open up the conversation or ask what it was her grandmother wanted to discuss. She would have to wait.

Alma hardly needed prompting to take seconds of the biscuits, slathering two more with butter and preserves and sighing contentedly. Her grandmother asked if she would like to take a walk in the garden with her, and Alma knew she was getting closer to whatever it was the older woman wanted to actually discuss. Alma nodded and finished her biscuit.

After she changed into jeans and a T-shirt, she joined her grandmother at the front door. The older woman led Alma around the grounds, pointing out the newer rarities she had planted in the beds around the house. Her grandmother had a particular fondness for daylilies, although she cultivated a little bit of everything. At least it had always seemed so to Alma, who had spent many summer days going from bed to bed, pulling weeds. While her grandmother would perform the chore herself in the absence of any eligible grandchildren, she was never one to let a free workforce go to waste. Alma's grandmother led her from the front-most gardens slowly around to the back of the house, where she still contended with the looming forest to maintain her claim to the ground she had cultivated.

When they came to the longstanding pond, with its weathered sculptures and picturesque water lilies, Alma's grandmother used the excuse of fatigue to get Alma to sit down with her on the marble bench nearby. Alma knew they were about to get to the meat of what her grandmother wanted to tell her. She waited patiently, watching the water flowing from the waterfall and listening to the birds nearby.

After a few minutes, Alma's grandmother cleared her

throat, taking her gaze away from the pond and directing it at Alma. "I want to talk to you about something, and I know you're not going to like it, but you should hear me out." Alma nodded. Her grandmother took a deep breath. "When you come into your abilities, there will be a lot of things you're going to have to cope with. Not just politics; your lack of self-control can make your new strength dangerous to you."

Alma fought down the urge to make a retort about herself control, knowing it would only result in an argument—and knowing her grandmother would carry her point eventually anyway.

"I know you don't like the idea of an arranged marriage, but you need a mate, Alma."

Alma shook her head involuntarily, mentally rebelling at even the suggestion of an arranged marriage. They had discussed the possibility before, though not with the level of seriousness her grandmother brought to the topic now. Alma knew that among elementals—particularly the higher echelons, the stronger elementals whose family line went back multiple generations—arranged marriages were not unheard of. It wasn't just a way for the ruling elite to keep the political climate stable, but a way to deal with unstable elementals themselves. Complementary partners were selected in the hopes they would give birth to elemental children and keep the powers contained in specific families instead of spreading them out. Powerful families often negotiated for years with other powerful families, brokering deals for daughters to marry sons at great benefit. Alma also knew her own grandmother had been in an arranged marriage with her first husband; when he had died, she had married Alma's grandfather, another elemental.

Alma's grandmother held up a hand to forestall a protest from her granddaughter. "You are going to need a mate, and you need to find one soon after you come into your full abilities. The elders nor the first families, will accept it if you go without a mate for too long. Not someone as powerful, and as unstable, as you." Alma saw the sadness in her grandmother's eyes. "Even if you were the most stable elemental on the planet, as powerful as you will become, you will be in danger from all sides. You need someone to give you balance, someone to protect you."

Alma gritted her teeth. She had learned to accept the basic fact of her natural instability—her flightiness and the extremes it led to—and had humbly learned how to rein in her temper and how to focus, at least a little bit, on subjects that didn't interest her.

"Grams," Alma said, forcing herself to speak slowly despite the denials and retorts that sprung so readily, poised to jump from her tongue. "I understand what you're saying. And I'm sure finding a good mate will help me achieve balance. But I can't stand the idea of an arranged marriage. I know you were happy with your first husband, but—" She took a deep breath. "—I guess I'm too thoroughly modern," she said with a little smile. "The idea of committing myself to someone I don't even know, even if they're perfectly complementary, is terrifying. I think it would make me much more unstable than I already am."

Her grandmother stared into her eyes intently and Alma tried not to flinch. She knew her grandmother wasn't looking at her. She was reading her lifeline, looking at the possible futures, peering into the abyss with her intuitive abilities. Finally, after a torturous moment, the older woman sighed and looked away with disappointment written all over her features.

"You'll find a mate, but I can see if I try to force it on you, it will never work." Alma felt a pang in her chest at having disappointed her grandmother, just as she always did. She wanted to retract her statement—no matter how true—and volunteer to allow her grandmother and attempt to find a suitable match for her. Now that her grandmother had taken the trouble to look into her future, however, Alma knew she had seen the potential for disaster. While she wouldn't acknowledge Alma was right about the potential for an arranged match to make her more unstable, Alma had to believe her grandmother had seen a similar fate—anything less dire than that and she would not have given in.

They continued their path around the lush gardens. Alma couldn't shake the sadness she felt having disappointed her grandmother, but she knew deep down there was more to the situation after the swift defeat her grandmother had allowed. Alma feigned ignorance as the older woman meandered through the plantation of trees at the back of the property before leading her around the house once more, talking about the troubles she'd had with some particularly difficult plants now blooming vigorously outsides of their usual climate. "You know, since you're here visiting, I could use some help weeding," her grandmother suggested as they approached the house. The clouds overhead boded ill for accomplishing any garden work that afternoon, but Alma knew by the next day she'd be outside taking care of the chore and she would probably volunteer without her grandmother needing to prompt her.

Alma thought more about what her grandmother said. Despite her refusal to agree to an arranged marriage, she knew that finding a mate was an important part of survival among elementals; particularly among those with any instability in their nature. It was considered vital to find a partner who could provide balance and steadiness. Her mother had been an unstable elemental, and she had gone into a semi-arranged marriage with her father, which had ended within ten years as the two became increasingly bitter and adversarial. As a result, Alma hadn't had any contact with her biological father since—one of the terms of the agreement reached to dissolve their marriage. Alma had never felt the lack of a paternal figure in her life, though; her stepfather had ensured that. Part of Alma's hesitation for finding a mate was due to the shattering end of her parents' marriage. She struggled to see marriage with any amount of certainty in the wake of that.

But Alma had been lonely most of her life. Sure, she'd made friends consistently throughout her childhood, but she had never found the rapport she sought with a lover. In all of her relationships, she'd found physical satisfaction but found herself constantly restless in every other way, ready to move on the moment the mystery was gone. Alma couldn't stand the sensation of feeling tied down, and she became annoyed with lovers she could predict too easily. She wasn't against having a partner; she simply wanted someone who would truly be a partner—someone she didn't feel weighed down by, someone she felt equal to. She often felt it would be nice to not feel so lonely, but she'd given up hope on the possibility of finding her equal.

That afternoon, as she did the grocery shopping and picked up the cleaning, Alma wondered what her grandmother would pull out next. She knew the discussion about her developing, soon-to-culminate abilities was far from over. There was no hint of a plot afoot when she returned, however. Alma decided whatever trials her grandmother had in store, she would have to deal with them.

three

The next morning when Alma emerged from her bedroom, she was surprised to hear voices coming from the kitchen—unfamiliar ones. She paused in the hallway, listening sharply as her grandmother spoke to the unknown guest.

"Thank you both for agreeing," she said. "My granddaughter is not as…concerned as she should be about the way things are in the community."

Alma frowned, wondering what her grandmother had gotten them to agree to and who these people were. The chill of suspicion ran through her. What had her grandmother done so quickly out of *concern* for her?

"You said she's been kept mostly out of the community since she was a teenager, besides meeting some people her own age," a softspoken, young-sounding, male voice noted. "It wouldn't be surprising for her not to know how tense things have gotten."

Alma was transfixed. She stood in the hallway, wanting to know, but hesitant to show herself.

"It shouldn't be too difficult," another voice said.

Alma felt the stirrings of anger begin. The idea that her grandmother didn't trust her with her own fate and had enlisted the help of two men for some unknown purpose without even talking to her about it cut deep. Even though she felt a little underdressed in her pajamas, she marched through the entryway into the kitchen and stared at the three conspirators as they sat at the table. Her grandmother smiled slightly, not even a little surprised at her appearance.

"Alma," her grandmother said, her voice pleasant and reasonable, "I'd like you to meet Finn and Dylan."

Alma glared at the two men, her hands unconsciously positioned on her hips. She assessed them quickly. They were obviously related—most likely brothers—and attractive. One seemed to be older, with medium-brown messy tufts of hair shooting out chaotically from his head. His blue eyes met her gaze with confidence. She stared back into his almost predatory, wolflike features. He was fit and filled out his T-shirt almost as well as the younger one. Their features had similarities—the shape of their jaw and lips. The younger, however, had a softer, gentler look to his face. His dark, brown eyes were less intense and his short, dark hair laid flat against his head.

"Have a seat, Alma. We were just discussing you." Finn gestured to an empty chair beside him.

Alma sat down away from the other three at the oblong table across the room, her arms folded over her chest.

"So I heard," she said tersely. She knew it wasn't fair to blame the men, but she couldn't bring herself to direct the fullness of her anger at her grandmother.

The older woman stood slowly and walked over to the

coffeepot, taking a mug out of the cabinet, and filling it before bringing it to the Alma.

"You'll have to excuse my granddaughter. She's not her usual sunny self this morning."

Alma took a deep breath and removed her gaze from the two men at the table as she added sugar and cream to her coffee, then stirred the concoction, forcing her temper under control with effort. Finally, when she had calmed herself, she looked up, taking a sip of her coffee.

"My apologies." Her tone was derisive. "So what brings you gentlemen to the house?" Alma forced her voice into a pleasant tone. A glance from her grandmother told Alma one person at the table at least was not fooled by the sudden change in her demeanor. Her grandmother smiled pleasantly.

"Since you are unwilling to find a mate, I asked the boys' parents if they would protect you as you come into your abilities."

Alma inhaled deeply, glancing from one to the other. The younger of the two men looked at her with a rueful smile, as if he understood her frustration. The older maintained a slightly proud expression, looking at her unemotionally.

"I don't entirely understand why it is I need protection, Grams." Alma fought to keep her voice neutral and polite despite her sense of betrayal.

Her grandmother sighed. "My dear, a lot of people would like you either dead or under their control, and that's the truth of the matter. You're too powerful already—once you transform, you'll be more of a target. The elders are already worried about you."

Alma took another sip of her coffee. She shouldn't be

lashing out at the men seated at the table, but they were the physical representation of her grandmother's lack of trust in her ability to take care of herself.

"So what are Finn and Dylan going to do to protect me?"

Alma's grandmother raised one well-shaped, dark eyebrow at the insolent tone of her voice.

"They're going to stay with you. I know you have plenty of room in your apartment for guests. I will give you money for their share of the rent, and they're going to receive some money for a living as well."

Alma opened her mouth to protest, but her grandmother continued. "They will be your bodyguards, day and night, until you find a mate."

Alma gritted her teeth, suppressing the first angry retort that came to mind. She took a deep breath and counted to ten mentally.

"Exactly how are they qualified to be my bodyguards? And why do I need two?" Alma could see her grandmother was enjoying her discomfort, amused by Alma's struggle to maintain her composure. The elder of the two also looked amused, adding gasoline to the fire building inside of Alma.

"You need two because you are liable to get yourself into trouble that it will take three people to get you out of." Her grandmother placed her coffee cup down. "Finn is a fire elemental who came into his full abilities a year ago; Dylan is his brother and a water elemental. Between the two, they should be more than capable of protecting you."

Alma recognized the tone in her grandmother's voice. There was nothing she could say to stop the plan from happening; her grandmother had already made up her mind. As the matriarch of the family, there was absolutely no way Alma could contradict the older woman. If she tried to fight it, tried to go against her grandmother's wishes, she would come under fire from her aunts and uncles. She felt herself becoming angrier, and as her rage grew, the wind picked up outside and Alma didn't care. Her grandmother knew she was angry; demonstrating her feelings, unconscious as it was, didn't make a difference.

Instead of arguing, Alma stood, abandoning her cup of coffee, and walked quickly out of the kitchen. She knew she would catch it for leaving so impulsively—her grandmother couldn't stand for one of her children or grandchildren to be rude—but Alma also knew if she stayed and tried to argue, she would only become angry to a point of losing control of her abilities. She let the door slam behind her and walked towards the woods.

The wind rose, howling shrilly through the trees, shaking branches, and sending dead leaves flying through the air. Alma looked up at the sky, her anger building as she thought how unfair it was she was being forced to live with two strangers set on her by her grandmother. She would have to accommodate them in her life, all because her grandmother didn't trust her to handle herself. She closed her eyes, listened to the wind, and willed herself upward. Gradually, as she focused on the task, Alma rose from the ground, rocked by the wind that continued to howl through the trees. She pulled herself up through the air slowly, opened her eyes and found the tree she had loved to climb as a child. She moved in that direction, focusing her entire will on moving through the air. When she reached her favorite branch, she let herself come to a stop with her feet above it. The venerable old tree had been her favorite haunt for years and when she learned to fly, it had only become more attractive to her. Alma wrapped her arms around and held on to the trunk of the tree tightly, not willing to exert the effort to bring the wind speed down. The tree swayed, and Alma let the movement gradually calm her down.

She knew she was acting immaturely, and her grandmother had her best interests in mind by providing her with bodyguards, but she had become frustrated with the fact that, in the elemental community as well as among her family, she was still seen as a child simply because she hadn't come into complete possession of her abilities. She'd managed to finish college and make a life for herself using the gifts she had been blessed with. She was financially secure. Just because she wasn't a "mature elemental" her family elders, and everyone she met in the elemental community, still treated her as if she was a teenager who needed to be protected and bossed around.

Alma was feeling sorry for herself when she spotted Dylan. He was walking towards her tree, looking around, and she knew he was looking for her. As he came closer, the concern in his face grew clear. He battled the wind she had unconsciously directed at him, and, for a moment, she felt her anger flag slightly. She knew she shouldn't be taking out her frustrations on him; he had merely done her grandmother a favor. He wasn't personally trying to mess up her life. Alma brought the wind speed down to a mere gust, but she stayed on the high branch, hoping Dylan would pass her by.

Instead, he stopped at the base of the tree and looked straight up. "You don't have to come down," he said, projecting his soft voice up to reach her. "I just wanted to say I'm sorry my brother and I are getting in the middle of your life. Your grandmother's friends with our nana, and when she asked us to do her a favor, we couldn't say no."

Alma abruptly felt ashamed of herself for her temper, hearing her grandmother's voice in her mind. "Nobody will ever take you seriously if you're always throwing tantrums." She sighed and looked down at Dylan, who was watching her for some kind of reaction. With a deep breath, Alma launched herself off the branch, and floated down between the tree's limbs until she landed a few feet from Dylan. He grinned. "That's not a bad trick," he said.

Alma chuckled. "It's saved me from injury more than once," she replied. She licked her lips subconsciously and appraised the man standing in front of her. There was something kind about his demeanor, something comforting and conciliatory. She extended her hand to him. "I apologize for acting like a brat," she said.

Dylan took her hand, shaking it quickly and firmly with a smile. "Trust me, I understand. My brother kind of has a temper."

Alma heard the wry amusement in Dylan's voice and decided he was understating the fact. Maybe it wouldn't be boring having the two men stay with her.

"Would you like me to show you around?" she asked, wanting to make up for her outburst. Dylan nodded, actually looking eager for the tour.

Alma led Dylan around the property, pointing out the different plants her grandmother cultivated and telling him about the summers she had spent there. Dylan listened attentively. They stopped at the pond, like she and her grandmother had the day before. Dylan watched the water in pure rapture, and Alma smiled to herself. They talked about their families, about growing up as elementals. It was strange to Alma how quickly she felt comfortable with Dylan, the easy friendship that seemed to develop between them already. Dylan paid attention to everything she said, listening silently as she explained why she was so upset about her grandmother's machinations. When she finished unburdening her mind, he told her he understood her frustration, but he could also see why her grandmother was concerned. The world of elementals was not as safe as it had been even ten years before.

"Powerful elementals are in high demand in some circles," he said, without specifying which ones. "Also, many of the older families are becoming more conservative, and there's a lot of friction between younger elementals. It's been a really tense time for everyone."

Alma found herself persuaded by the reasoning of Dylan's arguments, despite her lingering resentment of being treated like a child. She led him through the remaining gardens and back towards the house and was in much better spirits when they walked through the door. Her grandmother was still seated at the kitchen table, while Finn had made himself at home in the adjoining living room with a cup of coffee and a book. It was an oddly peaceful scene. Remembering Dylan's approach, Alma felt ashamed of herself for having stormed out, and for the exhibition of her ill-controlled abilities. Her grandmother gestured for her to sit down at the table, and Alma found her seat with the cup of coffee she had abandoned still there. Dylan had explained why her grandmother had specifically requested the two brothers to be her bodyguards; and that they had grown up mastering their skills much as she had, but with the added benefit of an interest in investigation. There were enforcers among the elementals, and he and his brother had been chosen by the ruling elite to be trained in that direction. Their abilities had been developed for protection and attack.

While Dylan was the calmer, more conciliatory brother, he was as equipped to protect her as his fierier, more aggressive brother.

"I apologize for leaving so rudely," Alma said, speaking slowly and swallowing the well of pride and resentment she felt. "I should have excused myself, but I knew if I stayed, I would have been tempted to argue and would have gotten angrier and lost control of myself."

Her grandmother stared at her sharply for a long moment, and then subsided. "I accept your apology," she said.

Alma heard the slight stir of movement behind her. A moment later Finn came into the kitchen, seating himself at the table with a grace Alma couldn't help but admire.

"I assume from your long absence you were showing Dylan around the property?"

Alma nodded. Her grandmother turned and favored Dylan with a faint, but genuine, smile. "Did she think to show you my pond?" she asked with understandable pride and comprehension for how much that feature would attract him. Dylan nodded, smiling broadly.

"You've done a lot of wonderful things around here," Dylan said with polite enthusiasm. "Our nana told me you were a master gardener, but I had no idea of what that meant."

Alma found herself oddly charmed by how Dylan and her grandmother were hitting it off; it seemed to her, from her experiences that water elementals seemed to get along well...or poorly. She was pleased to see, it was the former rather than the latter.

"Finn and Dylan will stay here until it's time for you to go back home," Alma's grandmother told her. "I thought it would be a good idea to give you a chance to get to know them both, and for them to get to know you, before you were outside of my protection once more."

Alma tried to find suitable grace to thank her grandmother for her thoughtfulness, despite the way the highhanded move still grated her. She knew there was no way out of the situation; she would let the men protect her, even if it was only from boredom.

four

Finn's first impression of the woman he and his brother had agreed to protect was that she was sexy, but difficult. When she walked into the kitchen, standing a few feet away with her hands on her full hips, looking defiant, Finn had looked her over covertly. She was a few inches shorter than he and his brother with dark hair, still mussed from sleep, tumbling down to her shoulders in an asymmetrical cut. Her big, dark-brown eyes were set into an intelligent-looking face with slightly full lips and arched eyebrows. He couldn't help admiring her curves. He was a functioning heterosexual male. The pajamas she wore clung to her breasts and hips but obscured her legs. Finn had torn his attention away from her, feeling his initial interest piqued, and recognized the attraction as a danger; he was supposed to protect her, not seduce her.

He had felt a little sympathy for the woman as her grandmother explained the purpose of his and his brother's presence in the house. Aware of her growing anger, he hadn't been surprised when she stormed out. It was what he would have done in the same situation. He wondered why her grandmother hadn't even talked to Alma about her idea before bringing him and his brother in to protect her. Alma's grandmother, who had insisted the two men call her Lorene, sighed as the wind howled outside. Dylan glanced uneasily at Finn, and Finn knew it would only be a matter of time before Dylan's impulse to smooth things over came about.

"I'm sorry, gentlemen," the older woman said, folding her hands and smiling slightly. "It seems as though I didn't calculate my approach properly."

Finn chuckled at the rueful tone in the woman's voice.

They exchanged pleasantries for a few minutes, and then Dylan's instinctive nature to be a peacemaker drove him out of the house. "Miss Lorene, I'd like to speak with Alma, if you think she'll listen to me," he said in his soft voice, and Finn hid his grin behind the coffee mug, taking a long sip. Alma's grandmother shrugged.

"I have no idea if she'll hear you out, but she's probably in her tree. It's a magnolia, one of the tallest trees on the property." The older woman locked gazes with his brother and Finn knew the two water elementals were exchanging mental images—a talent he envied slightly in his brother. When Dylan left, Lorene turned to him, looking at him for a few moments with an intent gaze that seemed to bore into his very brain. "You're a very different sort of person than your brother," she observed. Finn nodded, wondering in the back of his mind if the older woman thought that was a good thing or a bad thing. "You'll need to take care with my granddaughter. She's smarter than I think you've given her credit for, and tougher too. If she feels like you're interfering too much in her life, she will push you out of it."

Finn absorbed the advice for a moment. Lorene stood,

taking his coffee mug, and refilling it without asking whether he wanted more.

Dylan was absent for a long time, long enough for Finn to get restless and read in the living room while he waited for their return. If it hadn't been for Lorene's perfect calm, and the fact the wind had died down a few minutes after Dylan had walked through the front door, Finn would have gone to see how his brother was faring. He had perfect confidence in his brother's ability to convince almost anyone to cooperate and calm down. He had been capable of that very feat with Finn for years, arbitrating arguments between Finn and his other brothers, and suppressing the temper that raged more intensely in Finn's psyche as his fire-aligned elemental traits intensified. Finn had only gradually learned to calm himself down, to focus on completing tasks instead of leaping from one to another. "Fools rush in where angels fear to tread," his mother had told him time and again when one of his impulsive actions had resulted in trouble.

When Dylan and Alma returned, Finn noticed his younger brother had worked the usual magic on the woman. She was much calmer, and when she apologized right away, Finn sensed it was time for them to discuss matters. He resumed his seat at the table and watched Alma grapple with her lingering resentment at having to accommodate himself and his brother for an indefinite period. It will be good incentive for her to find a mate, Finn thought, as the younger woman accepted the stipulations her grandmother set. He and his brother would get paid for their services protecting Alma, with the added benefit of having a place to stay and very few expenses. When their nana had asked the favor of them, there had been no way to refuse it. They both owed Nana far too much and, as the center of the family, they couldn't turn her down without facing pressure from their parents.

So Finn and Dylan had flown out overnight and followed the directions to the house in the middle of the woods, with no real expectation of payment or a clear idea of what they would actually be doing to help. When the situation became clear, Finn was relieved to discover Alma's grandmother intended to finance their time protecting her granddaughter.

"It's not going to make you rich, but my first husband was an Earth elemental," She said with a faint smile. "He left me in very good financial standing. My second husband was a brilliant air elemental and did well for us too. I can afford to give you fair wages for your time."

They would drive down with Alma at the end of her stay at her grandmother's and remaining with her to ensure her safety until she found a mate who could protect and stabilize her.

Finn had been considered an unstable elemental since he was a teenager. He had much better control over his abilities than he first had. There had been a great deal of discussion about him finding a mate when he came closer to the birthday when he would receive his full abilities. His own nana had repeatedly suggested that he find a good earth-aligned woman and let himself be grounded by her influence. Finn had hated the idea from the moment it was mentioned and rejected it so continuously that everyone had given up. He knew there were still murmurs about his unstable tendencies among the ruling elite, but if he served a function among the elementals, they wouldn't push too hard. He'd had mostly satisfying relationships with women, although the lifestyle he led with his brother meant he never kept a relationship for long. He knew he had a habit of pushing women away when they got too close. In addition to his lack of desire to "settle down," he didn't like the idea of anyone other than his brother being close to him emotionally.

Shortly after everything was settled, Lorene asked Alma to show Finn around the property, since she had already shown Dylan that courtesy. Finn had little interest in gardening, but he was content to have the opportunity of talking to Alma alone. She agreed, after mentioning she should change into something other than pajamas. Finn tried not to feel disappointed. Alma's sleepwear piqued his interest. He'd had an intense sex drive as a teenager that had continued unabated when he reached his full powers as a fire elemental. If anything, Finn thought it had intensified. He waited for a few moments, talking to Lorene about the book he was reading.

Alma stepped back into the kitchen clothed and, for a moment, Finn couldn't help but stare. She was casually dressed, but the fitted jeans and thin sweater clung to her womanly curves even more thoroughly than her pajamas. She'd pulled her hair back, revealing the curve of her neck, almost inviting his attention. He took a deep breath and suppressed the attraction he felt, reminding himself once again she was looking for a suitable permanent mate, and his job was to protect her, not become distracted by the way her ass filled out her jeans. He stood from the table, gesturing for Alma to lead the way. Alma didn't spare him a glance as she went through the front door. "I'll take you out to the far corner and we can circle around," Alma said over her shoulder.

"Fine by me," Finn replied. He couldn't resist the impulse to glance down as he followed her, and had to still his lust at the sight of her ass swaying as she walked. He moved closer to Alma to abate his distractions. She pointed out different plants as they moved along, telling him about their significance. Finn had always considered gardening a somewhat futile pursuit—when he was outdoors, he much preferred actually doing something active: playing sports or at least hiking. But he was interested in Alma's explanations about why her grandmother had planted a particular bed in a particular location, so the plants would get the right amount of sunlight. She told him a story about how her grandmother would throw pennies around the beds to keep away snails and slugs, and how she would tell people she was paying the flowers to bloom.

Despite his general disinterest, Finn was impressed with the sheer abundance of growing things thriving in one place. Alma led him around to a tall magnolia tree, smiling faintly as she looked up through its branches.

"This has always been my favorite tree. I learned how to fly because of it," she said, glancing at him with a trace of shyness in her smile. "Grams always scolded me for climbing trees, but I never stopped."

Finn grinned, thinking about Alma as a child, defying her grandmother.

"Look," he said, reasoning it was a good time to have the discussion they needed to have, "I know you're not thrilled at having two bodyguards protecting you for however long you take to find someone." He licked his lips. "Trust me; it's not the assignment my brother and I would prefer either. And I, for one, think you should take all the time you need to find a mate, if that's what you want."

Alma shrugged uncertainly.

"But you must know it's not safe. I can protect myself pretty well, and so can my brother. He'll be even better at it once he comes into his full abilities, but an air elemental has a limited means of self-defense—" Finn stopped short as Alma turned to face him fully.

"Limited means?" she asked him, her voice deceptively sweet. Finn realized he had made a mistake. Before he could even think to correct it, he heard the wind rising around them. Finn wasn't afraid so much as he was feeling somewhat cautious, focusing his mind on his abilities. If he had to scare the woman in front of him, to show her who she was dealing with, he would, but he didn't want to actually hurt her. The wind continued to rise until Alma was moving, slowly lifting off the ground. She looked up at the sky and made several odd chirping noises, and Finn backed away, watching her closely. He felt the heat building up in his body as he focused his fire affinity, concentrating it into his hands. It was a difficult trick to summon fire on his own, instead of controlling it, but he was able to do it when sufficiently motivated.

A moment later, Finn was surrounded by howling winds and the cries of dozens of predatory birds, all appearing from what seemed to be nowhere. They surrounded Alma, hovering around her as she rose fifteen feet above him, glaring at him balefully. She held up her hand and the attention of all of the birds—ranging from small but dangerous-looking jays to hawks—turned their gazes upon him. "Would you call this limited?" she asked him.

Finn heard the challenge in her voice. He grinned, although the hawks looked formidable. There were no animals his fire alignment let him command close by; but he focused his mind on his hands, pouring heat through them, feeling his skin crackling. He rubbed them together quickly and with a snapping, shuddering roar of heat, a ball of fire appeared between them.

"Birds aren't too bad," he said. He maintained his grin. "But they're pretty easily defeated by fire."

Alma's scowl intensified and Finn saw the thoughts running through her mind. He knew she was trying to think of a way to combat the fire he had at his disposal. Not being water-aligned, however, it would be difficult. Finn directed more energy into the fire he held in his hands, growing the flames into a larger ball. He tossed the fireball into the air and caught it, even as the wind built up even more. He considered what he could do to impress upon his charge he was the one with the power in the situation. He didn't want to actually cause a fire or any injury.

He decided simply tossing the fireball wasn't enough.

"How would you defend yourself against a fully-fledged fire elemental when they can do this?" He threw the flames in her direction, keeping his focus to recall the ball of crackling fire back to his hands at the last moment. Instead, however, the wind shifted abruptly. A tunnel of gale force knocking the orb out of its trajectory and spinning it off. The same wind tunnel turned and came directly at him, pushing him off of his feet until he landed in the dirt. Looking with panic through the gale, Finn saw the fireball wheeling off towards the trees where it would set something ablaze. The wind had not just sent the fireball off its target, it had caused the flames to expand and the ball to grow twice its size. Not at all what Finn expected.

He struggled to sit up despite the torrent of wind that plastered him to the ground. He extended his awareness out to the ball of fire as it moved away from him faster and faster, heading for a wooded area. He grabbed for it with his mind, desperate to keep it away from the trees, and called it back to him, maliciously passing it close to the birds on its path back to his hands. The smaller birds fluttered, spooked, but in the next moment the hawks were descending upon him, and Finn had to hold the ball of fire over his head toward them off.

"What else have you got, fire boy?" Alma called down to him, and Finn expanded the ball of fire further, dodging the fearless dives of the hawks, who were followed by the smaller birds. Finn wracked his brain, trying to think of what he could do safely. It was only a matter of time before his brother sensed his predicament, and he wanted to make sure he had impressed a lesson on the woman he was supposed to be protecting. He had a sudden inspiration. Focusing on the fire in his hands, he changed its shape, lengthening it, seeing the new shape in his mind. He sharpened the angle of the pole the fireball had become, flattening it into a sword. He waved the sword over his head, dispersing the birds, though the hawks tried to get in around the movements he made. Finn struggled through the corridor of wind that shifted around him, trying to push him farther back.

He lifted the sword and continued to frighten away the birds that, despite their service to their air-aligned mistress, had enough self-preservation to want to avoid the fire. He kept low to the ground, to keep the wind from lifting him, and began slowly moving towards Alma, who was trying to move backwards despite her challenging look. He didn't know how he would get to the woman so high above him, but Finn told himself he would find a way. He avoided the birds and considered how to scare some sense into Alma, whose attitude was making him angry. He growled lowly to himself, thinking she had no idea of the dangers she was facing among the developed elementals in the world. Some of whom would be interested in either killing her or forcing her into an alliance. Her cavalier attitude was getting on his nerves and, although she was clearly a strong elemental, he was in full possession of his abilities; he had to get the better of her.

They stood at a stalemate, Alma's avian defenders avoiding the fire he held in his hands, though they had taken up posts surrounding her. She was still out of his reach, though. If she would let up on her flight for even a moment, she would be at his mercy. Finn knew he needed to distract her. He shifted the fire sword into one hand and directed his attention into the other, quickly forming a small but potent flame in his palm. He shaped it slowly, and then when it was what he wanted it to be, he threw it in her direction.

Alma's attention wavered, and the wind she had been directing at him disappeared abruptly, Alma's hand guiding it at the fireball to direct it away from her. She hadn't entirely been expecting the quick attack and took her attention off of her flight as well as her adversary. She fell toward the ground, barely catching herself before she hit the dirt. Finn rushed at her, intending to scare her without actually harming her. He wielded his sword as if to strike and called the fireball back toward him, dispersing the birds once more. He was a few feet from her before she marshaled her focus once more. She held out her hands, and his fabricated strike was cast aside by an intense gust of wind that pushed him away from her, dragging his feet through the dirt with speed.

Before either of them could think of a way to get the advantage, they were interrupted by a stentorian shout. The wind cut off abruptly, and Finn looked behind him to see Lorene and Dylan both approaching. He could see the anger on the old woman's face as she made her way more quickly than he would have thought she was capable of. Dylan looked disappointed rather than angry, with a faint hint of amusement in his eyes. Lorene stopped her headlong pace as she approached, her jaw set, and Finn suddenly knew why his nana had called the old woman the most formidable water elemental she had ever met.

The depths of her green eyes, staring at both Finn and Alma, held the mystery of an ocean, and he felt the energy crackling around them. "I don't know what the two of you were fighting about, but you will both stop it right now," she said sternly, scowling from one to the other. In moments, the world had gone dark, and Finn looked up to see enormous rainclouds overhead. Finn was on the point of apologizing when the rain fell, extinguishing his sword in an instant and soaking everyone to the skin a moment later.

Alma recovered before he did, and she approached her grandmother, her body language showing her to be apologetic. He saw her speaking but couldn't hear the quiet words over the beating rain. Dylan stood at the old woman's side, taking in the power the woman had shown in such a stunning exhibition. It was rare for water-aligned elementals to summon rain so quickly; Finn knew it took a great deal of focus. His brother could call up water by will, but he didn't have the focus or strength to coalesce the water in the air into rain.

Dylan gave Finn a sharp look, and Finn knew it was as much his responsibility to apologize as it was Alma's. He took a deep breath, pushing down his distaste for being soaking wet, and approached the old woman. Alma bristled as he came close, giving him a baleful look and shifting away from him. Lorene had softened slightly, and the rain was leveling off from a torrential downpour into something more manageable.

"I take responsibility for what happened," Finn said, pushing down his pride. "Alma and I got into an argument because I misspoke, and she became angry."

The old woman raised an eyebrow at him, staring into his eyes as if to read his soul. Finn bit his tongue against the retort that sprang into his mind and turned toward Alma, conquering his pride for a moment longer. "I'm sorry I said what I said," he told her. "I still think you need help defending yourself, but I didn't mean to imply you were helpless."

Alma's lips tightened and she glanced at him, her dark eyes sharp for a moment longer before she subsided under her grandmother's stern demeanor.

"I am sorry I didn't give you time to explain your stupid remark," she said. Finn bit his lip against replying, knowing it would only spark another fight if he gave into the temptation. The rain was abating completely.

"Both of you come inside and get out of your wet clothes," Lorene said, satisfied with their apologies if not happy. "And if I must break up another fight, there will be real consequences." Alma nodded, and her grandmother gave Finn a lingering look until he, too, nodded his understanding. Without another word, the old woman turned on her heel and walked back towards the house with Dylan, Alma, and Finn in her wake.

five

Alma was relieved when it was finally time to travel back to the city and to her own home. The few days she had spent with the two men had been interesting, but she was glad to get out from under her grandmother's vigilant gaze. Things had gotten no less tense between her and Finn, though she had developed a rapport with his younger brother Dylan. On the few occasions she had been forced to spend time with Finn alone, Alma had been silent, not wanting to either get into another argument with him or let him irritate her into another exhibition of her abilities. It frustrated her to no end that her grandmother had sent her on many errands with the older brother, for groceries or to pick up an antique a friend had put aside for her. Dylan seemed at home in her grandmother's house, and when Alma had taken him with her to retrieve plants her grandmother had ordered from a nursery, they'd had a good time on the drive to the next town over, comparing their taste in music.

Dylan tried to reconcile the two, acting as a mediator when the three of them were together. "Guys...," he had said at one point, exasperation creeping into his voice, "we're going to have to spend a lot of time together. You two need to sort out whatever is going on between you, because it's only going to be worse without Miss Lorene around."

Alma had doubted things would be worse. If her grandmother hadn't interfered, then she could have easily finished Finn's ambition to prove himself better than her. She realized it was dangerous to battle with another elemental, particularly when her abilities weren't fully formed and available to her, but the idea she was some helpless damsel, being protected by men, galled her. Dylan kept telling Alma when they were alone together his brother really wasn't that bad; he had a temper, and a slight tendency to speak before he thought, but he was genuinely a good person beneath that. Alma had shrugged off the description, thinking Dylan thought his brother was a good person; they were related, they'd had their whole lives to get to know each other. How the two men—as unalike as any two men could possibly be, with one fire-aligned and the other water oriented—got along so well was a mystery to Alma. One she thought she could happily unravel from a distance.

"You can't drive alone," Finn told her as they arranged to leave. Alma felt anger rising at his authoritative tone. "Even if we're following along behind you, there's a possibility someone could knock your car off the road or something worse." They sat at the kitchen table, the remains of dinner in front of them. While Alma's grandmother was the best cook she had ever met, Alma was no slouch in the kitchen, and had been prevailed upon to make the meal. Her grandmother pleading fatigue after a long day spent with Dylan in the garden.

"And what exactly would be helpful about having one of you in the car with me if I get knocked off the road? You're just as likely to end up injured as I am."

Finn shook his head. "There's safety in numbers. One of us will ride with you; the other one will take the other car and stay behind. We'll stop every couple of hours. Besides, we can switch off driving that way."

Alma set her jaw, trying to think of a way to argue against the plan.

Dylan's dark, soulful eyes locked on her. "Alma, it'll give everyone a chance to rest and everyone a chance to drive. It's a long way to your apartment from here. Plus, just in case we get separated, there will be someone with you."

Alma knew this was one decision her grandmother was content to let her make for herself. She finally gave in, not because she thought it was a good idea, but because she knew her grandmother would prefer it that way and she was tired of discussing it.

When they were finally taking their leave, Dylan packing away a few cuttings and plants her grandmother had insisted Alma take with her to grow on her balcony.

Alma felt oddly sad to be leaving, despite her increasing frustration and sense of restlessness. "If you found a mate that suited you," her grandmother whispered in her ear as they hugged in the driveway, "you wouldn't feel so restless and anxious all the time."

Alma bit back the irritated retort that rose to her lips, swallowing it down as if it were a pill.

"I won't remind you of it ever again, granddaughter, but

I must say one last thing; Finn is an eligible choice for you. He's come into his full abilities, after all."

Alma pulled back from her grandmother, shocked at the suggestion. She would sooner—if she had to pick between the two brothers—pair off with Dylan over Finn, no matter what temptations were offered to the contrary.

Her grandmother's green eyes glinted with amusement at Alma's revulsion to being paired with Finn, and the older woman gave her one last hug before turning back toward the house, discreetly dismissing her disdain for him. Alma shook her head in amazement and got into the driver's seat. Dylan was already settled on the passenger's side. Finn would follow her onto the highway, and they would make their first stop after two hours, at which point the brothers would switch.

By the time they arrived at Alma's apartment complex, all three were exhausted. Alma told both brothers tersely to leave the job of unpacking the two cars until the morning and led them up the stairs to her unit. She had reason to be proud of her living space. It had two floors, having been converted into a sort of inexpensive penthouse by the building management who had wanted to attract a higher caliber of tenant. She had a sprawling master bedroom up a flight of stairs with a small guest bedroom next to it and another bedroom on the first floor next to the kitchen. After giving her unwanted guests a brief tour of where everything was in the apartment, she told them to pick their rooms however they wanted; as long as they didn't disturb her, she didn't care.

Alma hoped Dylan would pick the smaller bedroom

next to hers. Although she wasn't attracted to him exactly, she found his presence restful, and she didn't want to deal with the tension of being in close quarters with Finn any more than she had to. Instead of waiting to hear what the two men would decide, Alma went into her bedroom and made her way directly for the bathroom. She didn't have her grandmother's water alignment, but she had always found a good, hot bath to be a therapeutic way to relieve her tensions, no matter what they might be. She started the bath, adding in the essential oils her grandmother had prepared for her and trying to push the arguments she'd had with Finn during the times he'd been in the car with her out of her mind.

It was impossible. The minute she sank into the hot water and closed her eyes, she heard his voice in her head. "It's no wonder your grandma is worried about you doing something stupid!" he had said when she had wandered away from the two protectors at a rest stop, interested in a cup of coffee and a few minutes of privacy. "Look, you might be a grown-ass woman, but there's a lot of shit you don't know about, and until you know, stop acting like such a fucking idiot." At another point in the drive, when they had been closer to their destination, they had fought once more about, of all things, who would pay for gas. "Jesus, woman, just let me pay. Your grandmother gave me money to help pay for the trip home, and that's what I'm going to use it for." At that point, Alma had been so tired and so irritated with the constant presence of the two men for the six-hour drive she had accidentally let her powers get away from her, the wind rising in the vicinity as she bickered with Finn at the pump. "What kind of fool turns down someone paying for them?" Alma had growled at Finn, livid without being sure of exactly why. "I can pay for my own damn gas, and I can take care of my own damned self. Go buy yourself some coffee or something. Christ! Leave me alone for FIVE MINUTES!" she had told him.

Dylan had, predictably, been appeasing by bringing out a cup of coffee for Alma without being prompted or even asking if she wanted it. Somehow, he had caught on to how she liked her caffeine, with just enough milk and sugar to make it palatable. While Finn stormed inside, Dylan was soothing her jangled nerves, mostly by agreeing with her that his brother was an asshole. *"He does have good intentions,"* Dylan had said mildly, giving Alma a slight smile. *"Most of the time, anyway. He just really, really sucks at expressing himself without pissing people off."* Alma had won the argument; she had paid for her own gas and instead of Finn in the passenger seat, she had Dylan, who had been happy to listen to whatever music she played. Finn had—predictably, Alma thought—scoffed at her desire to listen to country classics. *"God, this makes me want to kill myself."* He had groaned as Alma pressed play on the second album—more to spite him than because she wanted to listen to anymore. She had barely restrained herself from suggesting it would solve both of their problems if he did.

Alma grumbled to herself as the bath did not relax her. She sat up in the tub, scrubbing herself thoroughly and washing her hair until the dirty, grimy sense she had felt from driving all day was gone. She climbed out and wrapped herself in a towel, using another to rub at her hair as she stepped into her bedroom. She would have to live with the two men, she told herself firmly. If she wanted to shorten the duration of their time living in her house and tracking her every movement, the best idea would be to work on finding a mate. She felt as though she'd been maneuvered into that decision by her grandmother, and she resented that fact. If she really could find someone she wanted to be with, then it would be a double win.

Alma rummaged through her drawers until she found a pair of comfortable pajamas, then worked a comb through her hair, slowly untangling the snarls until she had calmed down as much as she was going to.

There was a knock at her door and Alma took a deep breath, reminding herself to be patient no matter what the situation was and no matter who was knocking. She walked the few steps to her door and marshalled all the patience she had at her disposal before opening it. Finn stood there, looking carefully neutral in a tight fitted polo. Alma raised an eyebrow in silent question.

"Dylan and I flipped a coin to decide who would sleep in the room next to yours," he said. Clenching his teeth briefly. "I ended up getting the room. I am no happier about it than you are."

Alma sighed, thinking to herself the day was a complete wash. She stepped back from the door slightly, letting Finn enter if he so chose; he came in and sat at her vanity.

"Do you need extra towels?" Alma asked politely, knowing although the two men were somewhat unwelcome, they were guests—and she had been brought up too properly not to ask, no matter how little she liked it. Alma looked at Finn for a moment as she pondered what more he could possibly have to say. When he wasn't actively being an asshole, she thought, he wasn't bad to look at. His eyes were a bright, clear blue, and his jawline was sharp but not too firm unless he clenched his teeth. His cheeks had light brown stubble across them, which lent itself to a slightly rugged look Alma was not immune to.

"We need to go over your schedule, so Dylan and I can cover you properly," he said.

Alma sat down on the edge of her bed and then thought better of it, her grandmother's suggestion about Finn's eligibility as a mate ringing through her mind. She stood quickly, glancing around her room until her eyes fell on the wingback chair she had moved into a corner months before and almost forgotten about. She couldn't remember why she had gone to the trouble of hauling it up the stairs to her room. The thought that she might need additional seating in her bedroom never crossed her mind.

She sat down, considering the question. She didn't have a set schedule. She had loose hours, part of the reason she had been so enthusiastic about freelancing. Alma remembered she had left her purse downstairs, with her phone still in it. She hadn't even considered when she would get back to work formally, so even the need for her alarm had not occurred to her. She thought back to the arrangements she had been working on when the trip to her grandmother's house had come up. There were a few clients she would need to speak to or meet with, to get information for her assignments.

Alma told Finn the few details she could remember, the potential meetings she would need to travel to the next day. It occurred to her she would have to bring one or the other of the brothers with her for the meetings, and Alma's dissatisfaction with the situation grew.

"We can talk about it in the morning if you'll have a better idea of things then," Finn suggested, surprisingly patient. "We're all tired."

Alma shrugged, thrown off-balance by the less antagonistic demeanor Finn had adopted. She wanted to be angry with him, particularly after the bath spent in remembering their arguments. But the man sitting at her vanity, facing her, was difficult to be angry with. He was paying attention, being respectful, and not cutting her off midsentence with an insult or a dig at her intelligence or common sense. Alma was suspicious. He stood, finally, yawning and turning to leave.

"One last thing," he said, the tension returning to him. Alma steeled herself for him to say something insulting or stupid—or both. "I want to apologize for being an asshole today. When I got the room next to yours, Dylan pointed out what a jerk I had been all day, and I realized he was right."

Alma shrugged. "Neither of us was at our best," she suggested charitably. The apology surprised her somewhat, though Finn's admission that Dylan had prompted it did not. Alma wondered why they hadn't just agreed Dylan would share the room closest to Alma, since she got along better with that brother. She supposed they had their reasons for determining it with a coin toss. "I accept the apology. I'm sorry I was acting like an asshole too."

Finn smiled slightly and turned away, leaving her room and closing the door behind him. Alma suddenly felt every bit of the fatigue she had earned during the day, and no amount of frustration kept her from turning off the lights in her room and gratefully climbing into her own bed, curling up, and falling asleep in a matter of moments.

six

Finn woke to the aroma of coffee and something delicious smelling cooking. He dragged himself out of bed, feeling as if he had slept only three out of the last eight hours, but telling himself that he was on the clock. It was to be expected he'd sleep lightly. He pulled a T-shirt on and left the guest bedroom he had taken, scrubbing at his face with his palms before he navigated the stairs to the main area of the apartment. The smell of mouthwatering food intensified as he made his way, and when he reached the ground floor of the unit, he saw Alma busily cooking and Dylan sitting at a barstool watching as she did something at the stove. Music played quietly from a speaker set off to the other side of the open kitchen. For once something he liked: alternative rock.

Finn sat down next to his brother in silence. The two nodded to each other in greeting, and Finn glanced at Alma. She was dancing slightly, oblivious to anyone else, focused on the task at hand. In the morning light that poured through the high windows, Finn had to admit she wasn't difficult to look at.

"My dear brother has joined us," Dylan said, projecting his voice above the music. Alma looked up from her work at the stove sharply, her features briefly wary and disappointed before she replaced the expression with a more neutral, polite one. She turned away from the work of cooking scrambled eggs and Finn watched her retrieve a mug from a cabinet, filling it with coffee wordlessly and depositing it in front of him, gesturing to the milk and sugar. Finn doctored his coffee and watched with amusement as Alma ignored him completely, diving back into her cooking and her enjoyment of the music. She was moving her hips, singing softly along, closing her eyes occasionally and nodding her head in time.

After a few minutes, she served up eggs alongside bacon and French toast on three plates. She deposited each in front of him and Dylan. Finn was impressed. He was generally useless to the world until after he'd had a cup or two of coffee and, although he knew Alma had excellent manners, he hadn't reckoned on such a spread for her unwelcome guests.

He accepted a fork and knife from her and started in on breakfast, wondering what motivated such a change in demeanor. Likely, he thought with a twinge of envy, his brother had been at work softening the stubborn woman. Finn had spent most of the time he was awake thinking of the variety of things he knew about Alma's situation and the importance of her reaching her full abilities—things Alma did not know. Her grandmother had told him certain things privately, outlining why it was so important Alma be protected until she allied with another elemental. Finn was glad he and his family had little to do with the politics of the elemental world. The stress of "wild" elementals had made things precarious for even the oldest families.

Lorene's instructions to him were to prevent Alma from being forced into an alliance with another family and to keep her from being killed. Considering some rivals Alma's family had, it could prove to be a challenge, even if he and his brother kept a watch on her twenty-four hours a day.

Dylan had made it clear to Finn it would be much easier to protect and defend Alma if he wasn't constantly offending her and picking fights. The fact that Finn was barred from telling Alma specifically what they were protecting her from made it difficult to bear when she insisted she was fine and could take care of herself. Alma had been sheltered from the darker parts of the elemental community, even as she had been trained for her place among the elite. She had only been formally introduced to the families Alma's grandmother trusted. Even in college, her grandmother had kept as many bad influences away from her granddaughter as possible, though she had told Finn sadly she hadn't been able to temper the girl's wild spirit before she had become a woman.

"So," Dylan said, pushing his plate aside when he finished eating. "What's on the agenda for today?"

Alma glanced at her phone, taking a sip of her coffee. "I have a meeting at eleven with a client who wants to introduce me to someone who needs a translation from Russian into Bulgarian," she said. "After that I am working at home all afternoon on translation work I've already lined up."

Finn glanced at his brother. One of them would have to go with her to the meeting. It would be better for both of them to go, but it would be much less conspicuous for Alma to have one more person as opposed to two. If one of them remained at the apartment, it would also let them guard against anyone sneaking in while she was away. Alma leaned against a counter and Finn knew she was waiting for them to weigh in.

"One of us should go with you," Finn said. "I'd say both of us, but that would be too obvious. Anyone watching you would figure out you're being guarded."

Dylan nodded his agreement.

"How well do you know the client?" he asked.

Alma considered it. "The one who contacted me, I know pretty well. I don't know his new client at all."

Dylan glanced at Finn, who shrugged.

"It could be nothing, just a coincidence."

Alma raised an eyebrow. "Are we really going to do this thing where we question everything that happens in my life?"

Dylan smiled mildly at the woman, and Finn took a deep breath, forcing down his impatience. "Since your grandmother hired us to protect you, we have to look at the worst possibility for every situation." He kept his voice level. "Which one of us goes with you?"

Alma looked from one to the other, her arms crossed over her chest. Finn noticed she wasn't wearing a bra and wondered, without meaning to, whether she was wearing panties underneath her pajamas. He pushed the thought away immediately.

"Well, you decided by coin toss last night, go for it." She collected their dishes and took them to the sink. Finn read her irritation and knew she was trying to suppress it, to channel it into more productive activities. He looked at his brother who shot him a grin and found a quarter in his wallet he had left on the bar the night before. Finn called heads, as he typically did; the quarter landed on tails. Dylan would go with Alma to her meeting. Finn tried not to be annoyed when Alma greeted the news with a satisfied smile. He knew she preferred his brother's company and he could understand why. It seemed as though if he and Alma spoke for more than ten minutes at a time, they had an argument, sniping at each other in irritation over some very unworthy topics.

Finn realized he was as much to blame as Alma for the arguments. The fight that started their relationship off had been a portent for how it would continue. Alma was fiercely independent, a trait Finn could appreciate and would normally have enjoyed, but her independent spirit could get her into trouble under the current circumstances. He had never again tried to impress upon her the limits of her abilities, particularly since she hadn't come into her full power as an elemental yet. But he had been tempted with every argument they'd had since that first day.

Dylan was the more suitable person, Finn told himself, as he settled in on the couch in the living room. She was meeting with someone she knew already. If the "new client" was someone suspicious, Dylan could handle the situation. If he wasn't, then he and Alma could come up with a decent cover, a reason for him to be there. When Alma came down from her bedroom ready for the meeting, Finn tried not to stare. She was professional looking, in a pair of dark-wash jeans, a subdued blouse, and a fitted blazer; but somehow although she was dressed conservatively, Finn couldn't keep his eyes from tracing her curves. His gaze lingered at her full bust, the way her hips moved as she walked across the floor in a pair of low heels. For a moment he was tempted to ask her to get something for him from the kitchen, solely to see her from behind. He conquered the temptation and turned his attention firmly back to the hockey game he was watching, even though he wasn't interested in the least.

Dylan came out of his room in a suitably professional looking outfit and he and Alma discussed what the cover would be. Dylan would be her assistant. Alma produced a notebook for him to write in while they met with the clients. They went over their cover story and Finn thought to himself that it stood as good a chance as any of working. Finn got involved in the planning before they left, taking Alma's phone from her, and programming his own cell phone into it as one of the quick dial contacts.

"Dylan's got me on his phone too," he said. It was an obvious precaution they took with every phone either of them ever owned. "If anything goes down, call me. Even if you can't talk. If I get a call from you, I'll know there's something going on and I can track you down from there." He didn't tell her he had a barely legal program built into his phone that would trace the location of her cell phone once it received her call. It wasn't important. He could track any number that called, and if Alma and Dylan were separated, it would do no good if Alma couldn't call.

Alma said the meeting shouldn't last longer than an hour and left with Dylan in tow. Finn tried to settle back into watching the game, but found he felt anxious despite the precautions they had taken. While Dylan had had no problems dealing with similar assignments in the past, Finn understood from his conversations with Alma's grandmother they were up against some heavy hitters—something Finn and Dylan hadn't really contended with before. The client they were seeing wasn't an elemental and had no idea Alma was. Finn knew there was no reason to suspect anything was out of the ordinary. In addition to the phones, Finn and Dylan had invested in fail-safes. They carried backup contact methods, so in the worst-case scenario, they could always find each other.

One of Finn's fire-aligned talents was tracking. He was a quintessential hunter, like the animals his fire abilities gave him the ability to control. Dylan had limited psychic abilities, which would doubtless become strengthened when he came fully into his power, but at the very least he could lock in on Finn's mind anywhere in the world. As teenagers they had tested the ability, increasing the distance gradually. He was able to "read" Finn and other people he was close to, in a limited sense, but didn't have any ability to communicate. Finn thought if Dylan got sufficiently close to Alma, between the two of them combining their power, they'd be able to get a message out telepathically.

Finn helped himself to another cup of coffee, trying to settle his uneasy nerves. He realized some of his disquiet sprung from the fact there hadn't been any attempt on Alma since he and his brother had arrived in her life. Of course, he told himself, they had only been away from her grandmother's house for a little over twenty-four hours. That was hardly enough time for someone to spring any real trap. His mind countered, if someone had been working on a plan before her grandmother had asked him and his brother to protect Alma, they should have already come after her. He flipped through the channels and told himself he was uneasy because he was in a stranger's home, and because he was out of control of the situation. He had faith in his brother. He reminded himself that Dylan had protected plenty of people before; they had acted as bodyguards on more than one occasion. While they may not look like the stereotypical bodyguard type, both of them athletically built rather than musclebound, they were sufficiently powerful to make up for it—and they were stronger than they looked.

Finn was finally convincing himself to relax. He looked at his watch, the meeting should've almost been over and then she would be home and under two sets of watchful eyes. He let his mind wander, trying to think of what he and Dylan could do to break up the monotony of their watch, when his phone pinged once. Then again. Seconds later it was ringing.

Picking it up quickly, Finn saw the text message from his brother just before it disappeared: SOS. The phone call was from Alma. Finn hit the intercept button to get her location before hitting the accept button to see if she was able to talk. If he could find anything out about their situation, at least he could locate her.

Over the phone he heard scuffling, and Alma's voice raised in strident protest. It cut out abruptly, the tone announcing the call had been terminated. "Fuck," Finn muttered. He called up the application that would track her phone's location. He hoped whoever had made the grab for her didn't know she had the phone on her. The application was automatically tracking his brother based on data from the contact patch they each kept on them. He watched the icon indicating his brother's location as it moved, while the one for Alma remained in one place.

Finn had to make a decision—the right one. Either they had dropped Alma's phone, leaving it behind before taking her or they had Alma in one place while they took his brother elsewhere. He wasn't concerned with tracking his brother; Dylan would handle himself. Their priority had to be Alma's safety. Whoever was involved in the situation may have separated them, and without a tracker on Alma it would be much more difficult for Finn to find them, especially without his brother. He could do it; he had the tracking ability, but it would be easier if she had the phone.

Finn grabbed his phone and the keys and rushed out of the apartment. He decided on the location where the phone was. If Alma wasn't there, he would track her with his other abilities and hopefully find his brother at the same time.

Finn cursed low under his breath as he got into the car and plugged in the phone, hooking it into the car's GPS and instructing it to lead him to the phone's location. He wouldn't have much time, particularly if the intent of Alma's assailants was to kill her. Finn pushed the thought away that they may have already, if that was their goal. He pulled out of the parking spot quickly and got on the road, listening dispassionately to the GPS directions echoing through the car's sound system.

seven

Alma felt like hell. She lay bound in the back of a van, seething with rage and powerless. She should have noticed something was amiss, she thought bitterly, taking refuge in anger to avoid the fear bubbling under the surface. The meeting had been concluding, everything had seemed more or less normal. She stood to shake hands with the new client and leave. The next moment, she felt herself suddenly crippled, pain shooting through her body. Alarmed, she had looked down to see an iron bracelet locked onto her wrist. The pain was intense, rocking Alma's body from head to toe. She saw Dylan stand when another person—one who hadn't been in the room before—came up behind him and murmured something before knocking him unconscious with some form of magic. The "new client" locked another iron bracelet on Alma's other wrist, intensifying the pain. She fell to her knees, groaning in helpless misery. It was a dirty trick, she thought, fuming as the two men gathered her and Dylan and carried them out. Alma's old client had left the room halfway through the meeting, saying he needed to attend to a business matter, but he trusted they would come to an agreement.

Alma quickly remembered Finn had put his number as a speed contact into her phone. She suspected he would track her but didn't know how. She gathered enough energy to dial out, and saw it connect. Her anger overcame her at that point and, as they took her and Dylan outside, she screamed to be let go, kicking and twisting despite the terrible pain that shot through her body every time the iron bracelets brushed against her skin. It was magic of an ancient sort—a type Alma had learned about but had never used. She managed one good kick at her assailant before he bundled her into the cleared back area of an unmarked van, reaching out for a pair of iron shackles. She kicked more vigorously. Her phone fell from her hands onto the floor of the van. Her assailant saw it and threw it out through the open door before falling on her and holding her down while he locked the shackles around her ankles.

Alma had time to reflect on her situation while the two strangers drove them away from her client's office, silent in the front seats of the van. Dylan still had not recovered, but Alma hoped he had managed to get word out to his brother. Even if he didn't, she thought angrily, she would find a way out of her predicament. Glancing at Dylan's unconscious form nearby, Alma knew she was responsible for him too. The iron bracelets made her ache bone deep, their ancient magic sapping away at her strength. For a while, she knew, anger would remain useful to her, would keep her energy up, but long enough in the restraints and she would fall into a helpless exhaustion. Iron, an earth-aligned metal, quintessentially associated with that element, had the power to "ground" any air elemental. The magic came from the magical associations that each element, and elemental, had. Since earth was in most ways opposed to air as an element, it pulled air down, so the magical items associated with it carried the power to sap the abilities and strength of air elementals. The pain was a side effect, a galling one in Alma's current situation. She tried to lie still, tried to push her sleeves down between her skin and the iron bracelets on her wrists, but it was no use.

As long as the restraints were on her, she wouldn't have access to her elemental abilities. Her mind would be the last thing to go. She would maintain her intelligence and her willpower the longest since that was so central to her being. But she couldn't call the wind, she couldn't call for the animals she had dominion over, she couldn't do any air-related magic while she was trapped in the iron. Alma's fear rose to greater prominence than her anger, and she felt a sharp panic. She didn't know the men who had taken her and Dylan, or what they wanted. She only knew they were elementals, or at least familiar with magic associated with elementals. Alma looked at Dylan again and wondered just what kind of spell the other man had used on him and how long would he be unconscious.

She had no way to keep track of how long they had been driving. Alma curled up, aching and becoming more and more exhausted as the iron pulled her down. Whoever had grabbed them, they knew what they were doing. She tried to keep her mind occupied with her mental list of elemental correspondences to distract her from the pain, thankful at least to have something productive to do. If they were fire elementals, she thought, she would find silver bracelets and anklets and somehow get them on the two men. If they were water elementals, she'd give them a taste of brass. If they were earth elementals, she would damn well wrap them up in aluminum foil if she couldn't find anything better.

Abruptly, the car came to a stop, and Alma opened her eyes. From her viewpoint on the floor, all she could see through the thin strip not covered on the back window were signs of a lavishly landscaped location, trees overhead. She heard the men in the front of the van talking to someone. While her mind wasn't as quick as it might be, she realized they must be talking to some gate guard. Alma struggled to sit up; the iron felt as though it weighed so much more than it must. She fought against it, breaking out in a sweat from the simple act of trying to pull herself from the floor of the van. She knew the longer the restraints were in place, the more difficult it would be, and the heavier they would feel. The van moved again, and Alma caught sight of the top of a gate they were passing through as the movement made her fall to the floor again too weakened to keep herself stable. She needed to get the restraints off. The sooner they were gone, the sooner she would regain her abilities.

Dylan was stirring when the vehicle came to another stop. Alma considered struggling with her assailants once more when they came to get her, but the effort it would take was next to impossible. Until Dylan was awake and aware, she was in too weakened a state to take care of them both. The best thing to do would be to get the restraints off, and deal with the rest afterwards. Dylan groaned, and Alma held a small hope he could help her soon.

The van doors opened. She cried out in pain when one of the men shifted her and pulled her toward the back opening of the van. Every minute the iron touched her was a practice in withstanding torture.

The other man grabbed Dylan and locked a gold

bracelet on each of his wrists. Alma knew she was in more serious trouble than she had first suspected. If they knew an elemental technique to quell powers, they were likely to know more. The question was, how they had known Dylan was a water-aligned elemental? This was a serious situation, and Alma's fear—and anger—intensified. She occupied her mind with thoughts of revenge as she and Dylan were lifted out of the van and carried towards a house.

The correct term for the residence, Alma decided as she got a better look at it, would be a mansion. It sprawled over a huge piece of land. The grounds were as well maintained as any wealthy Victorian would have them, with topiary and manicured grass. The house was brick and timber, a half Tudor style Alma would have admired more if it were not for the fact her assailants were carrying her toward it shackled. Her sluggish mind realized the men who had attacked her, and Dylan were not the ones in charge. She shook her head, trying to clear it of the deep, cold fog settling in, to no avail. As she was carried towards the house, Alma thought if she never saw another iron bracelet in her life, it would be too soon. She could consume iron as part of her diet, and with certain precautions she could use cast iron cookware, but from a young age, she had kept the iron in her life to a minimum. She hated that metal, and she had now more reason than ever for her hatred.

She and Dylan were taken into the palatial home through a marble foyer all gilt and ostentatious wealth. Alma pieced together if she had indeed been taken by elementals—and it seemed likely that such was the case—then the person in charge was likely an earth elemental. Alma yelped as she was deposited haphazardly onto a couch, Dylan was dropped in a chair not too far away. The two men left them there without a word. Alma felt anger overcoming fear thinking about two of them being so helpless. She looked over at Dylan, who was waking up from whatever spell their assailants had used on him. She pitied him once he became conscious and felt the pain of the fire-aligned bracelets burning away at him.

When Dylan came to completely, he let out a muffled groan. Alma tried to think, tried to force her mind into high gear. Whoever had come after them was not interested in killing them or they'd be dead already. There was some other purpose at play. Alma couldn't imagine anyone—even an elemental—thinking she would be a good target for a ransom attempt. While her grandmother was comfortable in her living, the person who owned this stately home was already far wealthier. For what purpose would someone kidnap her, then?

Her skin itched where the iron touched it. She fought the urge to scratch, knowing it would only become more intense until she had scratched her skin raw. She tried once more to push her sleeve down between the bracelets and her skin, to get some relief from the constant magical irritation of the metal.

After an undeterminable time, Alma heard movement from a distance. She and Dylan had looked at each other but had no way of knowing whether or not guards listened in to prevent an escape. Instead, they exchanged pleasantries while they both writhed with discomfort, speculating as to where they were and what would happen to them. Alma's mind had finally fallen on the idea that, if she could gather enough strength, she could try and unlock the bracelets on Dylan. The fire-aligned material would not affect her, just as the earth-aligned iron would not affect

Dylan. If she could get him free of his restraints, he might be able to use some of his magic to break her free.

A short man entered the room, immaculately dressed in a tailored suit. Alma stared at him as he approached. He wasn't awful to look at. He had dark hair and eyes with a medium-dark skin tone. He took a great deal of pride in his appearance. His hair was close cropped to his head, his face smoothly shaven, and Alma thought she saw the glint of manicured nails as he folded his hands in front of him, stopping a few feet away from where she and Dylan sat, trapped. He smiled slowly at the two of them, and Alma immediately resented him. He was undoubtedly the owner of the house and the mastermind behind her abduction. Even if what he wanted was reasonable, Alma was suddenly determined to make sure he didn't get it.

"Alma," the man said, coming closer to her. His voice was thin and reedy, surprising compared to his muscular build. "I'm sorry we had to meet under these circumstances."

Alma scowled at him, feeling the pain pulse through her system from the iron that felt like it was crushing her slowly but steadily. "If you're so sorry, then perhaps you will do me a favor and get rid of these stupid bindings, you asshole." Alma kept her voice sarcastically sweet.

The man shook his head, frowning slightly in a mockery of regret. "I'm afraid I can't do that," he replied. He seemed to take no offense to the name-calling. "I have to admit, you are even more beautiful than your pictures." Alma raised an eyebrow, wondering where the man was going with that comment. She tried to push back the fog filling her mind. It was affecting her mind more slowly than her body, but the iron was insidiously breaking down every last ability she had as a creature of air. She had to get rid of it somehow.

"Why should that matter?" Alma asked him. She took deep breaths, trying to suppress the pain she felt in every inch of her body. She didn't glance at Dylan, but she wondered what he was thinking, what plan he was coming up with. He was, after all, the one in the business of protecting and investigating people; he should know what to do in the situation.

"I have decided to ally myself with your family," the man told Alma, coming closer as he became more accustomed to her state of debility.

He was only a few feet away, within kicking distance. Alma tried to gather the strength to kick him.

"Or rather, I believe you will find it in your best interest to ally yourself with my family."

Alma managed a shrug, carefully controlling her face to keep the pain from showing on it. "I have no interest in allying myself with any family," she said, keeping her voice neutral. Her spite came back to the fore, and she continued. "Especially not with a family that has abducted me with a dirty trick and is uncivilized enough to keep me in discomfort in their home."

The man looked at her sharply, his dark eyes trailing over her face. Alma felt herself trembling from the pain and lethargy working on her and tried to marshal her strength, to keep her anger alive enough to keep it from showing.

After a long moment, the man came closer giving her a significant glance. "Out of concern for your well-being," he said, "I will remove the bindings on your wrists. I don't want you to run, so the ones on your ankles are staying to hobble you."

Alma felt a rush of excitement. The man hesitated at the last moment and withdrew a small box from his jacket pocket. He dropped to his knees in front of her. "This should be more romantic," he said brusquely, "but, I will free your wrists if you agree to become my betrothed."

Alma cursed in her mind, keeping her face steady. The man opened the box and revealed the ring. The stone was a stunning, huge emerald, set in a band Alma assumed was platinum from its intense brilliance. The platinum wouldn't do anything to her, but the emerald would limit her abilities. She thought to herself the man was a fool if he thought she actually intended to go through with it, and the emerald at least was not as bad as the bracelets she had on.

"I agree," she said, thinking to herself that she would very much enjoy if this man were killed. He put the ring on her finger and then touched each bracelet, murmuring something Alma didn't understand—a spell. One she had no way of learning. The bracelets fell apart and the man took them and slipped them into his pocket.

Alma's mind cleared slightly, and she shook her head, feeling as though she had been saved from being buried alive at the last moment. She looked up at the man who had coerced her into agreeing to an engagement and felt only anger for him. *Charm*, she thought, her mind gradually clearing itself of some of the malaise and lethargy that had come from the iron. She was still weak, still pathetically unable to put her abilities to use, but her mind was coming back to her slowly. *Charm him, and you might get some clue from him as to how to get out of this.*

"You know," Alma said, making her voice sweet and polite once more, "I never thought I'd agree to be engaged to someone whose name I don't even know." The man smiled, remaining on his knees in front of her.

"Phillip," he replied. "My name is Phillip Sall."

Alma nodded, fluttering her eyelashes slightly. She

licked her lips. "I must admit," she said, maintaining her sense of charm, "as irritated as I am from the way you've gone about getting me to agree, I have to give you credit for the intelligence of your strategy." Phillip smiled at the compliment.

Alma thought to herself how thoroughly she hated the man in front of her, and how very much she wanted to watch him die. Alma glanced at Dylan, saw he was watching them intently. "Do you think, husband-to-be," Alma said, licking her lips, "that you could arrange a private meal for us? There are some things we should discuss. I wouldn't want him to hear." She gestured to Dylan.

"Of course, my wife-to-be," Phillip said, more than contented now that he had gotten what he wanted with so little fuss. Alma felt the bile rising in her throat. "I will arrange that for us right now." Phillip leaned in and kissed her briefly on the lips.

Alma wanted to vomit. She pushed back the impulse and watched as Phillip strode out of the room, whistling to himself. She glanced at Dylan, who was still writhing in discomfort from the bracelets that trapped him. She wondered what the sensation was like for him—if it burned. She shook her head and looked down at the ring, deciding that even if it was an emerald, it was a pretty one, and probably worth a lot of money. Out of spite alone he would keep it even though she was most vehemently not going to keep the man who had given it to her.

Alma's legs were weak, heavy from the iron on her ankles. Instead of bracelets, they were actual shackles, and Alma wondered what kind of absurd dungeon her captor had raided to find them. She squirmed until she was at the edge of the seat and then fell to her knees, knowing she had to work quickly to do what she wanted to do. Alma crawled on her hands and knees towards Dylan, ignoring the pain that lanced up her legs with every movement. She focused on the end goal, on getting Dylan freed of the bracelets somehow and finding a way for him to help her out of the shackles. She reached him eventually, and stopped, holding herself up against the chair Dylan was seated in and catching her breath. Every shuffling movement had been like trying to pull a car.

Alma waited for a moment for the pain to subside and looked at the bracelets on Dylan's wrists. They weren't the same model as hers. She tried to get them off of him. She looked up into Dylan's brown eyes. "We have to be quick," she said. "He could come back any minute." Dylan nodded. Alma took the ring off of her finger and handed it to Dylan. "Hold on to this for me," she said. Dylan snorted, the pain in his eyes receding slightly as he appreciated Alma's thought process.

She studied the bracelets, trying to think of a way to get them off. With most of the iron off of her, and the emerald away from her body, her mind grew clearer. She tried to find a clasp, running her fingers along the metal cuffs. She almost missed it in her rising sense of panic, but she finally found the seam and slipped her finger around to the other side of the first bracelet. She flipped the inner catch, and the bracelet sprung open, freeing Dylan's wrist. She quickly worked on the other one as well and glanced at Dylan in amusement, slipping the bracelets into her pocket. She intended to keep those too, they might be valuable. Dylan shook off the lethargy and pain, and Alma could see he was trying to figure out what he should do.

Alma was stumped; looking down at the shackles, she couldn't think of a way in which Dylan's magic could remove them.

"I'll get you out of here, we'll find Finn and he'll be able to take those off," Dylan said. He shook his head. "My abilities aren't strong enough."

Alma nodded. They needed to get out of the mansion. As long as they could get away, they could take care of the rest between them. If nothing else, they could find someone who could break the chain or cut the shackles off.

Before they could decide on how to get out, however, Phillip was back. He spotted Alma on the floor, the ring off of her finger. His surprise and alarm turned into a deep scowl. "I should never have trusted the word of an air elemental so soon," he said, striding up to the two of them. Alma tried to move away, but the iron was weighing her down too thoroughly. Phillip grabbed her arm and pulled her up onto her feet. "You really think a water elemental will be able to help you?" he asked, his expression haughty.

The next moment, chaos erupted. What sounded like an explosion rocked the room from the other side of the door Alma and Dylan had been carried through. Dylan stood up quickly, reaching out and grabbing Phillip's arm, murmuring something under his breath Alma recognized as a spell. Phillip's grip on her loosened and Alma struggled to pull away, tumbling back onto the floor.

While Phillip's attention was on Dylan, she tried to think but the iron still clouded her thoughts too much. She shook her head, looking around. She couldn't reach out to the wind, she couldn't call upon any animals, and she couldn't use any of the spells she had learned over the years. Her heart pounded quickly, but her mind moved slowly. The intense pain in her legs radiated up from where the shackles gripped her ankles. Before she could put her thoughts together, Dylan was murmuring another spell. Alma watched as he pulled all of Phillip's strength from his body. He gripped both of his shoulders, while Phillip tried to wrestle him to the ground.

"Well, this is interesting."

Alma smiled faintly at the sound of the familiar voice. She looked beyond the two combatants and watched Finn stride into the room, a billow of smoke behind him.

Dylan and Phillip both looked at the new participant who stood several feet away, his bright blue eyes almost glowing as he took in the struggle going on. Alma wasn't sure if she felt relieved or annoyed at his presence. She and Dylan would have handled the situation.

Finn rubbed his hands together quickly and a fire sprung up between them, forming into a crackling ball. "Lot of nice stuff you've got here, Phillip," Finn said, looking as unconcerned as ever. "Be a shame for it to all go up in smoke like your door just did."

Alma pulled herself up onto her feet, gripping a chair for support. She gritted her teeth against the pain, wishing she could do more for herself than simply stand up.

Phillip pulled back from Dylan, apparently deciding the brother with the fire was the more important enemy at the moment.

"You wouldn't dare," Phillip said.

Alma wondered just how much magic Phillip had at his disposal and how effectively Dylan's spell had rendered him helpless. "I would have the police after you worldwide. There would be nowhere for you to hide."

Finn shook his head, tossing the ball of fire idly and catching it. "What would you tell them? That three elementals destroyed your house with magic because you kidnapped two of them. I can see that holding up... particularly once the elders hear about it."

Phillip was shaking with rage and Alma thought

someone in the room finally understood how she felt. She shuffled heavily, the iron shackles rattling as she did, echoing the jolts of pain every movement sent shooting up her legs.

"Phillip." She kept her voice strong. "You should have known better than to chain up an air elemental."

Phillip didn't look at her, too captivated by the threatening fire Finn was wielding.

Alma looked around and found a heavy vase. She gritted her teeth and picked it up, glancing at Dylan, who was gathering water around the two of them, condensing the vapor in the air into a fog to protect them from his brother's pending attack. Alma smiled to herself despite the pain she was feeling, the weakness continued to spread up from her legs.

"Hey, Aid!" she called out, hefting the vase in her hands. Finn glanced at her, raising an eyebrow at her use of a nickname.

"Don't call me that." He formed another orb of fire, not taking his attention off of Phillip.

Alma could see the wealthy earth elemental was considering his options. He crouched down and murmured. Alma realized what he was going to do; he would call to the earth underneath the home, start a localized earthquake that would knock them all around—all except for Phillip.

Dylan was too absorbed in his spell to do anything to prevent it. Finn saw what the man was doing and pulled his arm back, a fireball in hand. He launched the flames toward Phillip as Alma made her move. She heaved the heavy vase and brought it down as hard as she could against the back of Phillip's neck, falling to the ground next to him as she did. The fireball hit the chair beside them and lit almost instantly. The only thing that prevented the heat from affecting Alma was the cloud of vapor that surrounded her.

Alma struggled to get up knowing that, water vapor shield or not, she needed to get away from a fire that would quickly consume everything it could. Finn rushed toward her, and Alma looked down at Phillip, who was unconscious on the floor.

"Get these off of me right now!" Alma said to Finn, pushing her feet towards him. Finn looked down at the shackles. Dylan directed water toward the fire Finn had started, putting it out. Finn knelt at her feet and took the chain in his hands, murmuring. An intense heat rose between Alma's ankles. A moment later the chain parted.

She wasn't free, the iron still constrained her, even if her movements weren't limited by the chain. Still, she was relieved that freedom was in sight. Impulsively, Alma reached out and wrapped her arms around Finn's shoulders. She pulled him in close and kissed him hungrily. The heat generated between them was intense and for one moment she reveled in it. They tripped and fell to the floor together. Finn pinned her against the rug, kissing her back with burning tongue and lips, his hands traveling over her body in quick, devastating movements that left Alma breathless.

Dylan shook them and cleared his throat. "We should probably get out of here, don't you think?" he asked, pointing to the smoke still coming into the room from the hallway Finn had entered by.

Alma pushed Finn away from her, remembering in a flash she disliked the fire-aligned elemental in spite of his handy assistance in the previous moments. Dylan lifted her from the ground into his arms and gestured for Finn to lead the way.

They walked through the smoldering hole that had been the impressive front door.

"Did you take care of the other people on the property? Because they could probably detain us." Alma felt comfortable in Dylan's strong arms, though she would never admit it as he carried her toward the car.

"Oh, they've run off," Finn said, gesturing toward the gate the van had brought them through.

Alma looked in the direction he had pointed and saw that, like the door, it was smoldering wreckage. She nodded, satisfied.

"We could have handled ourselves, you know," she said tartly, not wanting to admit Finn's presence had been helpful, or that he had been right about her safety. If Dylan hadn't been there, if Finn hadn't been on their heels, she would have been in trouble. Her pride didn't allow her to admit to them she might not have gotten out of the situation.

Finn snorted. "You could, you know, thank me."

Alma rolled her eyes. "Please. We'd have figured it out without you blowing everything up."

Dylan chuckled, his arms shaking as they held her. He got her into the passenger seat and climbed into the back while Finn climbed into the driver's side. Alma shifted in the seat and shuddered at the pain still affecting her from the iron that held her ankles. She also felt intensely embarrassed at kissing Finn the way she had. What had come over her?

"Yes," Finn said sarcastically, starting the car. "I'm sure my brother could have carried you all the way to civilization and you'd have found a welder or something to cut those things off of you."

Alma crossed her arms over her chest, scowling at Finn.

"I didn't say WHAT we would have done, just that we would have figured it out. You could have taken the actual shackles *off* of me, you know." Alma couldn't take her mind off the kiss she and Finn had shared; it was seared into her memory. His hands had glided along the curves of her body with ease, his touch hot even through her clothes, his lips and tongue intense, awakening a sudden lust inside of her Alma knew she would have easily given in to if Dylan hadn't interrupted them. She wondered what Finn thought about what had happened—if he was even thinking about it.

Finn drove them quickly off the property. Alma tried to get comfortable despite the iron ankle bands and settled for sulking, trying to push the memory of Finn's kiss out of her mind. Instead of losing the thought of it, she found she was taking the kiss to its inevitable conclusion in her mind, thinking of what would have come next. In spite of her distaste for him as a person, Alma was consumed with curiosity as to what Finn would look like naked, and how the sex would be. She snorted privately to herself as her mind supplied the most obvious adjective: fiery and hot.

eight

Finn lay in his bed staring at the ceiling, trying unsuccessfully to seduce sleep. He couldn't get the kiss with Alma out of his mind. He had driven the three of them back to Alma's apartment and removed the shackles, throwing them into a dumpster outside when Alma vehemently declared she never wanted to see them again. He came back to find Alma seated at a desk in the living room of her apartment, hard at work with a cup of a restorative tea in hand. Dylan had turned on a football game, and for a while there was peace in the apartment.

But Finn hadn't been able to focus on the game. Instead he was remembering the way Alma had felt underneath him, how her kiss had lit something incandescent inside of him, a response he had never experienced with another woman. He had forgotten about the situation, about his brother standing a few feet away, about Alma's would-be fiancé knocked out next to them. For that moment, Alma had been the center of Finn's universe and all he could think about was bringing her pleasure, hearing her moan, feeling her writhe beneath him, and discovering if her body was as gorgeous as he had suspected. He had wanted to burn the clothes off of her and take her right there on the floor, with no more concern for propriety than had he been an animal himself. When Dylan interrupted them, Finn had fought the urge to blast his own brother away, his intense emotion driving him to a possessive madness.

Finn turned over in his bed, knowing there was only more danger to come. He knew Philip Sall would now have a vested interest in Alma's inheritance as an elemental, and there was little the elders in the elemental community would do about the situation. In their viewpoint, Alma was up for grabs, particularly as an unstable elemental whose best qualities would be better kept under firm control. He shook his head, burying his face in the pillow that smelled too much like Alma for his peace of mind. He had to make sure nothing ever happened between them. He knew he had to discipline himself. Even his brother would be a better partner for Alma than he would, Finn thought with a slight sadness. The thought of anyone having the woman sleeping only yards away from where he tossed and turned was repugnant, but he would have to stand for it—have to encourage it. Alma needed to ally herself with someone as powerful as she was.

Finn resolved to himself to push her away thoroughly. If she ever tried to kiss him again, he would prevent it. If she pursued him, he would make himself repulsive to her. They were bad for each other, and they would be even worse for each other when Alma came into her full abilities. Both of them unstable, neither of them willing to compromise or give in. It was a recipe for disaster. Maybe he should court some elementals, form his own attachment and encourage Alma to do the same. Finn thought about it, turning over once more and pulling his face free from the sweet-smelling pillowcase. He took a deep breath and told himself he would broach the topic with his brother the next day. Alma would take the suggestion better from Dylan than she would from him.

Finn finally fell into a light sleep, plagued by dreams of the woman he knew he couldn't have. Images of rescuing her again and again and again fluttered through his mind; instead of kissing him and then berating him, however, in his dreams Alma didn't stop kissing him. She spurred him on, the flames of Finn's desire consuming them both until they were completely satisfied.

He awoke during the night, covered in sweat from a vivid dream. Deciding he wasn't likely to get back to sleep soon, Finn headed downstairs for a midnight snack and maybe to get some reading done. He stopped on the stairs between floors when he heard voices.

"You were a lot more important than you realize," Alma was saying, her voice softened. "I should have kissed you, not your jerk of a brother." Finn heard the familiar sound of his brother's chuckle.

"I can't say I would have minded if you did. Considering how you two were going at it, you must be a good kisser." Finn felt bile rising up in his throat. He told himself if Dylan managed to attract and hold on to Alma, it would be good for both of them.

"How is it the two of you grew up in the same household, but you're a joy to be around, and he's a constant pain in my ass?" Finn was certain that Alma was flirting with Dylan.

"He's the older brother; he's always been that way. But he's really a good guy, Alma. I know you don't see it, but he is." Finn forced himself to turn around and move back up the stairs, his heart burning and his head aching as he realized the two people downstairs were establishing a rapport he could never manage. He turned on a bedside table lamp and read in bed until he was too exhausted to stay awake. He was more determined than ever to make sure Alma would find someone worth attaching herself to. And Finn decided out of pride, and just a little spite, that he would find someone himself. He would never let Alma know how intensely attracted he had been to her in that one moment—how easily he could have given himself to her. He knew it was better that way.

nine

Alma woke from a sound sleep—her entire body jolted as if she had fallen out of bed. She opened her eyes as the power surged through her body. The darkness of her room was evidence that dawn was still hours away.

She groaned in annoyance. The surge didn't hurt. Instead, every nerve in her body felt as though it were cranked to the max. The wind picked up outside and she grimaced, knowing it would take all of her focus to subdue it. She felt every thread of the sheets as they touched her body, heard the hum of electricity throughout the house. As the power surge continued, the wind blew harder and beyond her control, even as her sensory overload intensified. She covered her ears and tried to curl in on herself, but it was useless; the elemental power working its way through her body was building.

She heard movement downstairs in Dylan's room and in the guest bedroom next to hers. Finn should have been sleeping, instead she was uncomfortably aware of his tossing, turning, and muttering in his sleep. Not to mention

Dylan's faint snoring. The wind rattled the windows and whistled along the nooks and crannies of the apartment building. Alma tried to focus, tried to assert the control that her grandmother had taught her over the years. It wasn't working.

As the energy igniting her system peaked, Alma screamed uncontrollably, unaware that she was. The energy was too much—she couldn't handle it. Her mind felt fragmented in millions of pieces. A thousand thoughts whirled through incoherently. She wasn't sure which was worse—the wind, the sensations in her body, or the visions invading her mind. She was so overwhelmed that she barely registered the sound of her bedroom door opening among the sounds of the building creaking, the wind howling, and the sound of footsteps racing up the stairs. Still screaming, ignoring the pain in her throat, she tried to rid her body of the sheets.

Outside, the wind grew more intense. Alma tried to focus, the part of her mind not dealing with the onslaught of power knowing that a windstorm would be a rather conspicuous thing in her suburban town, that she should be more concerned about the possibility of creating a small-scale natural disaster than the unendurable sensations she was experiencing.

Her screams heightened in pitch as she felt hands gripping her shoulders tightly. She didn't want to open her eyes, terrified of what she might see. In spite of her return to normalcy after her kidnapping two weeks earlier, Alma had been jarred to the core by the experience. The iron she had been exposed to had taken more than a day for her air-aligned body to recover from. Her usual self-confidence had been shaken.

When she opened her eyes to the sudden bright light of

her bedroom, she expected to see a stranger, someone ready to cart her off to yet another suitor—or to someone who wanted her dead because of her abilities. The touch of the hands on her shoulders burned, and for a moment Alma's panicked mind couldn't process what she was seeing. The wind blew harder, and a crack of lightning exploded outside. Bright blue eyes bore into hers, medium brown hair rumpled with sleep, and as another loud crack of lightning reverberated overhead her mind realized it wasn't an attacker holding her against the mattress. Alma recognized that Finn had her by the shoulders and was pinning her down. Looking around wildly, she saw Dylan hovering behind his brother. The intense light burned her eyes, just as Finn's touch burned her skin. Alma closed her eyes tightly, turning her head away from the deafening sound of Finn's voice shouting to be heard over the wind.

"Alma! Focus!"

Instead of giving her an anchor, however, the energy from Finn's fiery grip only increased the power surge—heating her body, intensifying her sensations. She screamed again, struggling to get away from him.

She didn't notice Dylan push his brother away, but she felt the sudden coolness of Dylan's hands on her shoulders. He held her down and, instead of yelling, she heard his whispers as an undercurrent of the screaming wind. She felt herself weighted down. Everything calmed down. Her screams eased and were replaced by gasps for breath instead. Cold invaded every cell of her being and, with no effort on Alma's part, the wind began to gradually die down until it was a mere gust against the window. As the cold infected her body, Alma felt her senses attune to the sensations she had found unbearable only moments before. With deep breaths, Alma felt her racing heart slow. The moments of sensory overload, when she hadn't been able to think straight or turn her mind to the point of actually understanding what was happening, diminished and allowed her to assume a level of coherence. She heard Finn's voice, his words, where before she had only heard sounds. When he had held her down, he had been shouting for her to focus, for her to calm down, telling her she was safe.

Alma opened her eyes slowly, taking another deep breath. When she realized she was half-naked, the sheet wrapped around her the only thing keeping her from being indecent, her face burned with embarrassment, and she pulled the sheet to cover her completely. Dylan released her shoulders and stepped back. Finn hovered behind him.

She sat up slightly, smiling sheepishly. "So," she said, not meeting either man's gaze, "how about that crazy weather we've been having?"

Finn squinted his eyes curiously and Dylan stared at her as if trying to decide whether or not she was serious. She was somewhat relieved when Finn laughed and both men relaxed. Dylan sat down on the edge of her bed and Finn sank at the foot, both of them continuing to chuckle in relief that the crisis had apparently passed.

"Power surge?" Finn asked finally, raising an eyebrow. Alma nodded slowly. She hadn't experienced anything like it before—or at least, nothing so intense—but she knew what it was immediately. Her arms and legs continued to tremble, an electric sensation rushing through her nerves. Dylan's intervention had slowed things down, had subdued the powerful elemental energy thundering within her, but it wasn't done with her yet. Alma wondered how much more of the changing she would have to take, if the sensations in her body would become her new normal. Would she ever not feel constantly distracted, alerted by random movements of elemental energy in her body? Alma had been looking forward to assuming her full abilities as an elemental, but the prospect of more moments like the one she'd just had wasn't exactly enticing.

"Yeah. Hey—why didn't anyone warn me that could happen?" Alma felt her fear transform into annoyance. Even though she knew anger wouldn't solve anything, and if she let it go too far, she'd likely start another windstorm, she couldn't help feeling resentful that something like that could happen and no one had thought to warn her.

"Well, you are a powerful elemental. For most people going through the adjustment, it's not that...intense," Dylan said. "Finn only lit his bed on fire accidentally twice before he came into his full abilities." Dylan threw his brother an amused grin.

"At least I'm not likely to flood the house," Finn shot back. "Or wet my bed."

Dylan rolled his eyes. Alma was suddenly uncomfortably aware of just how naked she was under the sheet. Plus the fact that the two men sitting on her bed had seen at least her upper body exposed. While she had grown accustomed to a certain level of unavoidable intimacy in sharing her house with the two bodyguards, she hadn't considered the possibility of them seeing her naked in any capacity. Aside from the moment she had, in an ill-timed impulse, made out with Finn. She fidgeted, glancing down at the sheet as her face burned.

"Why don't you get dressed. We'll have some coffee. It's technically morning and I don't think any of us will get any more sleep anyway." Dylan gave Alma an understanding smile and stood, glancing significantly at his brother. Finn glanced at Alma once more before following his brother out of the bedroom, closing the door behind him.

Alma sighed, taking a moment to absorb the mortifying situation and all of its implications. She ran her fingers through her hair, shaking her head. She still felt the influence of Dylan's calming magic, but she was—as he pointed out—wide awake and unlikely to get any more sleep. Fortunately, she thought, the freelance nature of her work meant that if she was exhausted in the afternoon, she could take a nap.

She slipped out of bed, trying not to think about how exposed she'd been or the two very attractive men who had seen her basically naked. They could infer the rest from what they had seen. She pulled on a pair of pajama pants and a T-shirt, roughly finger combing her hair before she pulled it back into a messy bun. Alma considered not going downstairs for a moment, cherishing her solitude in the room and avoiding the awkwardness of the situation, but she had never been a coward and she didn't intend to start. She took the stairs slowly, still experiencing the tingling in her body, and still hesitant to be around the two men, despite her hype about courage. The aroma of coffee brewing urged her on.

Finn sat at the breakfast bar and Dylan moved about the kitchen, doing something while the coffee brewed. Alma sat down, feeling self-conscious and graceless. Finn glanced at her over his shoulder and sat back, giving her an understanding smile. "Dylan's right, you know," he told her. "I literally lit my bed on fire twice in the week before my birthday."

Alma snorted, wondering how he had dealt with that situation.

"The people at IKEA were amused and pleased to see so much of us that week." Finn smiled.

Alma chuckled, imagining the embarrassment of the situation. It made the events of a few moments ago seem slightly less mortifying.

"Didn't we tell them we had started a B&B?" Finn asked Dylan.

Alma laughed harder, picturing the two men sheepishly standing in an IKEA and lamely asserting that they needed another new bed because they would run a small hotel out of their home.

Dylan poured coffee, taking the milk out of the fridge, and passing Alma the sugar. "I think we did! I don't think they believed us, but they couldn't really question us too hard about it."

Alma doctored her cup of coffee, shaking her head. "Probably thought that one or the other of you was having energetic sex and just didn't want to admit it."

Finn dropped the spoon in his hand, spilling sugar everywhere and staring at her. "Why didn't I think of that?!"

Dylan took the milk carton from his brother's lax grip and poured some into his coffee, rolling his eyes. "Because no one would have believed that story either."

Alma almost choked on the sip of coffee she had taken, avoiding breathing it in only barely. She swallowed and gave Dylan an approving look.

"You know, it's a good thing for Finn you're a water elemental, you can help heal that burn you just gave him."

Dylan chuckled. "What should we have for breakfast? It's my turn to cook anyway."

Alma relaxed, realizing that neither brother would bring up her nudity. Dylan made bacon, eggs, and toast, and the three of them ate companionably, chatting and drinking coffee until the sun came up.

Alma went about her normal routine, working on her assignments while Dylan and Finn amused themselves playing music and watching television. "You know," Alma said, glancing up at the two brothers playing guitar a few yards away, "I'm entirely in the wrong line of business. I should become a bodyguard and lounge about all day."

Finn grinned and winked at her unknowingly.

Dylan put his guitar down. "One of us could go grocery shopping for you, or run some other errand," he suggested.

Alma sighed. It wasn't that she minded their presence in her home—not anymore, anyway—as much as it was that she was still waiting for the other shoe to drop. Dylan and Finn had accompanied her on her meetings with clients, one waiting in the car while the other went in with her, pretending to be her assistant. She conducted a good bit of her business from home, but before their entrance into her life, she'd had a thriving social circle. While they hadn't forbidden her to go out, having two men with her at all times would be conspicuous. She considered it a bright side that she wasn't spending as much money and she was earning plenty, staying up late to work extra assignments from sheer boredom.

"You can go out, you know," Finn said, divining her restlessness in one of the odd moments of rapport that existed between them.

Alma smiled slightly. "I know. It's just I can't think of a good way to explain two guys hanging around me all the time with neither of you being my boyfriend."

Dylan chuckled. "You could say you're working for the CIA and we're your shadows, to make sure you don't reveal state secrets."

Alma rolled her eyes. "And then I'll be plagued with questions—and at least one of my friends will distract Finn from the important task of guarding me with his life."

"Oh really?" Finn perked up.

Alma shrugged. "I don't have ugly friends," she said, closing her laptop. She wanted to leave the house; she wanted to go out and get drunk and take a cab home. Alma realized that part of the cause of her tension was not just that she didn't see her friends anymore—it was that she wasn't seeing any men, or at least not romantically. While she hadn't entertained any serious relationships in years, Alma had enough charm that, combined with striking looks, she convinced most any man she was interested in that he should come home with her—or take her back to his place. It wasn't the most emotionally fulfilling way to live, but Alma enjoyed the challenge, and the light touch of an attractive man who was no more interested in happily ever after than she was.

"I won't get distracted," Finn protested. "It's not like I haven't ever seen beautiful women before."

Dylan snorted at his brother. "I've seen you go through condoms. You'd get distracted."

Finn scowled at his brother. "I take my job seriously. Have you ever seen me neglect my responsibilities because of a woman before?"

Dylan considered the question. "No. No you have not."

Alma got up to get herself another cup of coffee. The predawn wakeup call was making it difficult for her to get through the day, on top of being restless. She had always been an active person, a trait that had intensified as she had developed into her elemental abilities. Being cooped up in her house, leaving only to run basic errands or to visit clients, was taking a toll.

A few days after the kidnapping that had finally given Alma a good sense of just how much danger she was in, Finn had suggested that she look around the message boards that elementals participated in, to see if she could find potential partners that way. The suggestion was sound, but Alma had balked at it. She knew such boards existed. She wasn't even surprised to find there was a matchmaking site for elementals, but the thought of going on blind dates expressly for the purpose of finding her mate was irritating. It reminded Alma too much of old-fashioned methods like arranged marriages—one of the tactics her grandmother had suggested when Alma had first balked at the suggestion she needed a mate.

In light of the power surge she had experienced in the early morning hours, however, and after a couple of weeks of curtailed social activity, Alma was considering the idea with a more open mind. Finn and Dylan were discussing something as she sat down at her desk and sipped her coffee, opening her laptop once more and using the cover of their chatter to navigate to one of the elemental forums. She filled in the form to join, knowing that tech savvy elementals had put systems in place to make sure that only elementals could enter the site. There were family tree verification requirements that would keep the "normals" out. Alma sighed as she received the message she would be notified within twenty-four hours as to whether or not she was accepted into the forum.

Well, at least I can go run errands with the brothers, she thought. She hoped they could be sweet talked into taking her to the mall for a few hours.

ten

Alma received a confirmation email before nightfall. After telling Finn and Dylan—sheepishly—that she had joined, both were in favor. Apparently, they were both active on the forums; they had to be, as part of their job.

"There are some really good people on there," Dylan assured her. "Maybe you'll find someone to hang out with."

Alma shrugged off the idea, though she had thought of similar reasons for joining. She didn't want to get her hopes up. But since the power surge had abated, Alma dwelled more and more on her sense of restlessness—and an underlying dissatisfaction at her celibacy over the past several weeks. The reckless kiss she'd shared with Finn hadn't faded from her consciousness as much as she wanted it to. While Alma knew any physical involvement with Finn would be a bad idea, her grandmother's hint notwithstanding, she couldn't rid herself of the impression it had left on her.

As she, Dylan, and Finn wandered around the mall from store to store, Alma's mind continued to get caught up in the brief but consuming passion she had felt the moment his lips met hers. She kept telling herself she didn't want to repeat it, but she had never experienced a connection so involving in her life. She had discussed it with Dylan privately, on more than one occasion after the fact. She wondered why she couldn't just develop feelings for the younger of the two brothers; he was so receptive, so patient, and such a good ear for anything she wanted to talk about. But there was no spark between them—there wasn't that passion Alma felt for his brother.

Alma had been distracted all afternoon, thinking about the way it felt when Finn pressed against her. She firmly denied the possibility of an attraction to the man himself, though she had to admit he was not unattractive from an objective standpoint. She stood firm in her insistence that she was not interested in him. She was interested in sex. She blushed as she realized that her libido was more active than it had been before and wondered just how much the power surge affected that change. She wanted to charm someone, to flirt and give him a knowing smile and cock her hip just so, to lure him into her bed. She wanted—needed—to get laid, and that was all there was to it. The difficulties associated with a one-night stand were a little frustrating, considering she would have to be guarded by Finn and Dylan, but Alma was determined to overcome them.

That night, Alma logged into the forums and introduced herself in the appropriate thread. She didn't say much—only that she was an air-aligned elemental, that she lived in a general area, and that she was getting used to her abilities in an adult setting. She had enough caution to know better than to reveal her lineage, or that she was about to come into full possession of her power. Dylan and

Finn added her as a friend on the system and commented on her post, solidifying her entrance into the social group. Alma had not avoided elementals as she had entered adulthood; one of her close friends was an elemental too. But she had slacked on networking with elementals her grandmother had introduced her to through her teen years. For the most part, Alma had tried to live as normal a life as her abilities would allow. She knew, not only from her grandmother's reports but also from Finn and Dylan's confirmation, that elemental politics had become fraught and tense.

She looked around the forums, reading posts and trying to get a feel for the different personalities. Some people lived in her area, and Alma responded to threads about things to do, clubs to visit, bars that were worthwhile. She knew she should be cautious, and at first, she kept that necessity at the front of her mind; after all, she was a target. She wasn't going to be targeted by most of the normal population, who had no clue that elementals existed; she was an object of interest for certain elementals. Even those elementals without a vested interest in her due to the strength of her lineage would be interested in her because of her strength. Although Alma hadn't given her relative power much thought as she had grown up, the surge that had awakened her, and occasioned a brief local news story about a freak windstorm, had made it impossible to avoid the realization she was more powerful than most of her family members at least.

Alma felt as though her newfound sense of caution was chafing her. She remembered the kidnapping. The knowledge she had been disarmed, captured, and carried off relatively easily, gnawed at her. She had never been the type of person to doubt herself, but in spite of her cavalier attitude, she felt more vulnerable than ever before in the wake of the kidnapping.

Out of anger, she'd sent a scathing email terminating her relationship with the client who had put her in a position to be kidnapped. There was no way to be sure how much her former client knew about the designs on her, but his willingness to put her in danger at all had made her indescribably angry. Anxiety was a familiar feeling for Alma, but rarely had she ever known direct fear. The sensation was frustrating.

When she swallowed her pride and told her grandmother what had happened, she endured the sigh of disappointment and waited for the lecture she knew would come.

"You need to find a mate," her grandmother had repeated. "If you had taken my advice, you wouldn't have had a problem from that man."

Alma bit back the sarcastic retort that fought to escape. Knowing the man had wanted to marry her only to secure her power for his own ends didn't make her feel too charitably towards the institution of marriage.

She recognized that her grandmother was ultimately right. If she found someone to enter into a serious relationship with, it might defray at least those in the elemental community who saw her as a commodity rather than a person. Alma told herself she wasn't looking for a husband when she posted in the forum, but she was open to meeting someone—a boyfriend who could entertain her and maybe take some of the pressure off.

That night Alma talked at length to a local elemental named Alex. He claimed to be air-aligned like her and live only a city away. According to his profile picture, he was rather appealing. Six feet tall and originally from England, he had a lean, almost hungry look to his face. His bright blue eyes and dark brown hair framed an intensity that both startled and intrigued Alma. The next day, she took breaks from her work to chat with him. Like every air elemental Alma had ever met, he was charming—a trait they all embodied. She knew her own flirtatious abilities had more than once been called devastating. It was nice to talk to someone who could keep up with her banter. Although she wanted to maintain her reserve, she opened up slightly. She talked about her grandmother without naming her, told him about her childhood spent learning to control her abilities.

They exchanged stories about their childish displays of power, about the times their precocity had gotten them into trouble and talked about their families. Finn chatted with Alex's cousin under the pretext of investigating the man Alma was talking to. Alma's libido, along with her curiosity, were piqued. She even blushed when he addressed her as "Air" in spite of the fact that she normally hated the nickname. Alma knew she should be careful. She, of all people, knew how dangerous a charming person could be. But that didn't stop her, she wanted to have some fun in her life. She entertained no illusions that Alex was "the one," but the idea of having fun with him was appealing. Finn's conversations with Alex's cousin, Dolores, had veered from checking out a potential date of Alma's to something more akin to a flirtation.

Dylan seemed to be the only one of the three questioning motives. "Don't you think it's a little bit suspicious?" Dylan asked Finn, making a slight face "I mean, no offense to you bro, but it's kind of our job to suspect anyone who's overly interested in getting to know Alma. I mean, basic precaution, right?"

Finn dismissed the concern. "It makes sense. Besides, Alma's supposed to be looking for a mate. If someone's interested in her, we should guard her, obviously—and take precautions—but if she can't be allowed to talk to someone, then she's never going to find a mate."

Alma shrugged when Dylan looked at her for her input. "Obviously we can't assume everyone is safe, but we can't assume everyone's a threat either, can we?"

Alma tried to read the look on Dylan's face. It wasn't disappointment or anger, it was concern. "I have no interest in being kidnapped again, but I also have no interest in staying put and just hoping everyone will decide there's no point in either killing me or forcing me to marry them."

"At least, if you meet up with these two people, make it a public place, and bring me along. I can be objective."

Alma looked at Dylan for a moment and wondered if some of his concern might be due to him being lonely. Since Finn had chatted with Dolores, Dylan had been left more often to his own devices.

eleven

They arranged to meet with the cousins for lunch, two days before Alma's birthday. Alma was also hoping she would like Alex enough to convince him and his cousin to attend the party she was planning for the evening of her birthday. She would travel back to her grandmother's house a few days after her birthday, but she wanted to celebrate reaching her full abilities beforehand. She never mentioned to Alex it was her "special" birthday, instead letting him believe she had already reached her full power as an elemental. She knew she needed to be careful around him, even if she found herself attracted to him and the easygoing charm he radiated in their chats. She admitted to herself that she was hungry for attention from men.

In the midst of planning, Alma received a letter from her grandmother. The handwritten envelope was a surprise. Everything was put aside. If her grandmother wrote to her, the contents of the letter were important. She'd tried to convince her grandmother to embrace technology, but the older woman refused to get used to chatting online, or even email. On more than one occasion she'd stated the phone was her personal limit for technology. She even still kept printed books and magazines for her gardening, instead of looking online. "Oh, I'm impressed and awed at how far things have come," she told Alma. "And I'm glad that you're so well versed in how to use the newest technology, but I don't have the patience to learn it myself."

Normally Alma's grandmother called when there was something she wanted to say. Letters were reserved for communication that required more privacy than the phone offered or for topics she wasn't comfortable speaking about verbally. Alma wondered which of the two categories the letter would fall under.

Considering in the lingering danger—and that her grandmother had been the first one to be cognizant of that danger and insist on protection—it seemed odd that she would choose such an archaic form of communication, one that could be intercepted easily. Then again, Alma knew their code was hard to break and would look like nonsense to anyone else. She tore into the envelope.

Dearest Granddaughter,

You would probably prefer a conversation like this in person. However, I've never been comfortable talking about these kinds of things directly in the flesh, as they say. There is a part of your transformation into a full elemental that I wanted to explain to you. I had hoped that you would find a mate before it came time for your birthday, but since you haven't, I thought a word to the wise would be a good idea. You are going to experience very strong—almost impossibly strong—lust as part of your transition into your full powers. As you approach the day of your birthday, it will intensify and on the night of your birthday, it will be at its most intense. I want you to be very, very careful about who you spend your time with within that period. If I did not think that Dylan or Finn were safe choices, I wouldn't have them with you, but think carefully about any other partners.

Alma felt herself blushing; she had noticed an increase in her libido, as her grandmother said. She kept reading.

I considered advising Finn and Dylan, but Finn, I assume, would know already and I trust your intelligence and sense of self-preservation. Please remember that as an unstable elemental, you are more likely to find it difficult to control yourself. I love you, and I look forward to seeing you once you've assumed your full powers; I still have a great deal to teach you.

She set the letter aside and considered the message. Alma told herself she had no interest in either Finn or Dylan. She was sure even a sharp increase in her libido, beyond what she was already experiencing, would drive her into either man's arms. Talking with Finn about it crossed her mind. He would know what she would experience—but she was wary of talking about her sex life with him. She considered going to Dylan. He wouldn't be able to empathize with her from experience, but he was the person she trusted most.

She thought about it more and put the concern aside until she had a better idea of what the extent of the problem might be. Feeling her cavalier attitude returning, she assured herself it was possible she could control her lust just fine. Even if she couldn't control her lust, what would be the worst possible outcome? She would satisfy it with some man she didn't care about and move on with her life, in possession of her full abilities. If she could not disconnect herself from a situation like that, she would consider herself a poor elemental.

Alma worked hard over the next two days to get as much work done as possible; she didn't want any assignments hanging over her head for her birthday, or for the week following it. Dylan and Finn amused themselves practicing guitar and martial arts, playing video games and watching TV—and in Finn's case, talking to Dolores. Alma tried to ignore the slight stab of jealousy his attention to Dolores incited.

She reminded herself she had no interest in him. Just because he had the dark-haired, light-eyed look she preferred in men, and just because his every touch against her skin sent a burning, sharply desirous sensation through her body did not mean she had any intention of inviting any advances from him. Not that he made any. She thought about that fact as she glanced at him grinning and typing away on his laptop.

Watching him, she considered how from the time she had been safely extricated from the earth elemental who kidnapped her, Finn had been increasingly distant. He avoided being alone with her, avoided talking to her at any length about any serious subject. In fairness to him, Alma realized her actions—grabbing for him and kissing him hungrily in the ecstatic aftermath of achieving her freedom—had implied she was interested in him. He was communicating that what he saw as her interest was not reciprocal. Alma tried not to let it bother her, despite knowing she had never failed to charm a man she wanted. *I'm not interested in him,* she reminded herself.

She had to believe her lack of a social life was driving her crazy if she was regretting men she didn't even want to be involved with. That can change—will change, she thought. Once she came into full possession of her abilities and learned how to master them, she knew she would be a match for anyone who might come after her. She would let Finn and Dylan remain her bodyguards, but she would not curtail her activities anymore.

Alma contacted her friends, working out a plan for her birthday. She wanted to go out, drink, and make a fool of herself. Approaching twenty-three, she knew there would be few opportunities left to enjoy being foolish and getting drunk. She wanted to enjoy the time she had left before she was consumed with responsibilities or a "mature" relationship with a "stable" elemental who would likely get her pregnant in a matter of months. The idea of "settling down" had always been an enigma to Alma, and never more so than when it loomed and seemed more necessary than ever before.

She planned an evening to rival the level of partying she had achieved during her college days. The evening's festivities included her favorite bar, which hosted karaoke on the night of her birthday eve, a strip club, and an afterhours location she had only partied at rarely, but knew stayed open until almost dawn. Dylan and Finn could handle her security, and she knew she didn't need to worry about a ride home—Dylan was responsible enough to make sure they got home in one piece.

Alma thought it would be nice to invite Alex, if he didn't turn out to be less interesting and charming in person than he was over the computer. She and Finn would meet him two days before her birthday celebration, which should be ample time for him to clear his calendar and have the night free, if she decided she wanted him to be part of her revelry.

The four of them—Finn, Alma, Alex, and his cousin Dolores—were going to meet for lunch. The prospect was inviting, and Alma didn't even need to consult her lust to know that a desire for intimate contact was strong inside of her. She was tired of being careful, of avoiding her social life fearing being attacked or kidnapped. She wanted to live a little, to enjoy herself.

twelve

Finn woke up during the night, frustratingly aware of the stillness of the apartment around him. In the days since being awakened abruptly by the sound of Alma's screams, he had found himself repeatedly jolted from sleep with the anticipation of another crisis. He remembered coming into his full powers and the week before that birthday. He had told Alma about lighting his bed on fire twice, but he had not told her about what had provoked the fires. He wondered if he should talk to her about one of the side effects of the power surging through her. He had experienced it himself. The lust he had felt starting a week before his full possession of fire abilities had never abated. He had learned to control it, to push it aside when it wasn't convenient, but he knew it would take something very intense to satisfy the desire he still felt.

The two times he had lit his bed on fire, he had been in a deep sleep. Dreaming. The first time, Finn had found himself in an impassioned argument with a woman whose face was not clear to him; no matter how many times he recalled the dream, he could never remember what she looked like. When he tried to remember what had started their argument, he was never able to. The dream began in the midst of the argument, past the point where something as mundane as cause was irrelevant. He and the woman were shouting at each other for no real reason, simply venting their frustration. In the dream, Finn felt his anger transform into something else: pure, unadulterated lust. He had no idea what his connection with the woman in his dream was, but there was the suggestion they were involved somehow—though the idea was vague. He reached out and grabbed her, silencing her words with a deep, passionate kiss. The woman in his arms froze for an instant in shock, and then her body relaxed against him. She responded, deepening the kiss as her hands explored his body.

The heat rose inside of Finn. He knew he should control himself, pushing it back, but her touch made it impossible for him to do anything but give his inner fire free rein. He peeled her clothes off slowly, his hands too slow for what he wanted. With a rising sense of urgency he needed her naked immediately and in his arms, her skin pressed against his, every inch of their bodies touching. He wanted to be inside of the woman he had been arguing with just moments before, to feel her power surging through him; somehow he instinctively knew that she, like he, was an elemental.

He had managed to get her naked, to touch her exposed skin, when the smell of smoke woke him out of the dream abruptly. Finn's eyes opened to flames rising around him, burning the sheets and the frame itself, digging into the mattress. He contained the fire before it reached the walls or floor, but the bed had been destroyed. The dream had remained with him. His want for the woman he had been fighting with, their passion for each other, was something that still stimulated everything within him. It was exactly what Finn wanted—a person who wasn't afraid of him, a woman willing to stand up to him, who would fall into his arms when his mind shifted from frustration to lust. The woman he had been wanting his entire life, only available in his dreams.

The second dream had been similar. He had been dreaming of a woman whose face he couldn't see—in this case, they weren't fighting. He was comforting her. Finn had never been comfortable with the prospect of extending comfort, but in the case of the woman in his dreams, he had put forth the effort, murmuring things he couldn't remember the next day, touching her and soothing her grief. He couldn't remember what she was upset about, what it was that had caused her so much pain. But he knew she trusted him—completely and totally—by the fact she would cry in front of him. He had wrapped his arms around her, and she had turned to him, pressing her lips to his in an impulse he could understand. The kiss transformed from an expression of the woman's need for comfort into something deeper; she was touching him everywhere, her warm tears rolling onto his face. Her hands, small and deft, slipped under his shirt, and Finn knew that the comfort she wanted was something much more visceral and much less gentle than he had been giving her.

Once more, clothing was shed and both of them were touching each other, hungrily kissing every spot their lips could reach. Finn had been so turned on it was agonizing, his whole-body tense with anticipation of release. The smell of smoke had pulled him out of his deep sleep, and once more the bed had been destroyed. The incidents had since stopped, not because he had gained control of his abilities, but because Finn's dislike for lighting his bed on fire prompted him to wake up from the increasingly erotic dreams before they became so intense that his abilities kindled everything around him. He had never been able to recognize the woman in his dreams, but Finn knew if he ever met her, he wouldn't be able to handle himself. He would have to have her—he would have to win her, convince her that no other man could give her what he could. Of course, remembering that resolution, he knew it would be a good idea to keep his fiery impulses under control to avoid lighting another bed on fire when, and if, he won the woman of his dreams.

Thinking about the dreams distracted from the larger point. His lust had been nearly insatiable and was still difficult to control. Alma would go through the same thing. He had never asked what happened before her power surge. He wondered what she had been dreaming of and he suspected it would not be an isolated incident.

He recalled being yanked from a relatively sound sleep by Alma's screams and rushing into her dark bedroom as the wind howled outside. Seeing her thrash around the bed, struggling against the power running through her body, Finn knew at once what she was experiencing. He recognized the agony of the sensory overload and being consumed by the energies transforming her body, everything so intense. He had acted without thinking, pinning her down to the bed, trying to get through to her; in retrospect he understood his mistake thoroughly. It still grated on him that Dylan had been better able to calm her than he had. In fact, in some respects, he thought he had somehow made it worse, judging by the lightning strikes that had occurred while he'd had her pinned down.

One part of that night replayed in Finn's mind. He had

purposefully avoided mentioning it, and had even tried to avoid thinking about it, but the image of Alma sprawled out on the bed, her body exposed to her hips, leaving little to the imagination, had remained with him. The sight of her breasts moving as she panted, her creamy skin, the pale, dusky pink of her nipples, was forever impressed in his mind. He had never known Alma slept in the nude; he wasn't even sure it was a normal occurrence for her, but having her in the room next to his and knowing she might be had been in his mind every night since.

He had been trying to suggest Alma take a more proactive approach to finding a mate; but after that night, he couldn't help the surge of jealousy at the thought of any man having full access to her curves. He told himself he was simply a connoisseur—that he appreciated her body as a lithe, nubile woman. But he knew if he was honest with himself, he was perilously close to losing his objectivity about Alma.

When she had hesitantly told him and his brother she had joined one of the elementals-only forums, he had been both relieved and a touch jealous. She could find someone there more suited to her personality. Despite his increasingly difficult-to-ignore hunger towards the woman, Finn knew deep down he and Alma would not make a good couple. He distanced himself from her after the night he rescued her, when he had overheard her talking to Dylan in a way he realized was more flirtatious than friendly. Nothing had come from it, which confused Finn. His brother was objectively attractive and had a lot to offer a woman. But Finn also knew that all air elementals found it as easy to flirt as they found it to breathe. Emotionally, he felt a little bad for Dylan because his brother hadn't felt confident enough to press his suit. He hadn't broached the topic, but Finn knew that it would be difficult for any man that Alma had her sights on to ignore her or disregard her charms.

When Finn investigated Alex's family, he had no intention other than probing to see if there was any possibility of danger to her. However, Finn quickly found himself drawn into Dolores's subtle, wry charm. Dolores had used the wits that embodied her air alignment that Finn's interest in information was more than casual. He had not admitted he was set to guard Alma until she found a mate, but he admitted to a sort of brotherly interest in her well-being. *"Our families are close,"* he had explained to Dolores. *"I've known Alma since we were kids and I just want to make sure...you understand."* It was a little lie, but he reasoned that if a time for the truth came, Dolores shouldn't fault his intentions.

Increasingly Finn chatted with Dolores, not just to get more information about the family—what kind of politics they were into, their position among the elementals, things that might raise a red flag—but because she was interesting to talk to. Both Alex and Dolores were musicians, like his brother and himself. But they had made a living from their music. They performed in separate bands that often toured together throughout the United Kingdom. A year before they had settled stateside, wanting a change of pace and were happy to find things "less stuffy" in the US for elementals, as Dolores had put it. When she had suggested they chaperone the first meeting between her cousin and Alma, Finn had been happy to agree, interested in meeting the distracting woman in person. He welcomed her high energy and humor. He needed something to take his mind off of the woman he was guarding, to keep him from compromising himself. When

Alma mentioned she was thinking of inviting the two cousins to celebrate her birthday, assuming all went well at the first meeting, Finn was happy to give his consent.

Dylan, Finn noticed, was less than pleased with the development. Finn understood his brother's position. It wasn't entirely safe for them to encourage Alma to meet new people, particularly elementals. But it was also part of their responsibility to see that Alma found a mate successfully. Her safety in the world of elementals depended upon allying herself with another family, or at least another person of good standing in the community. Once she did, there would be fewer attempts to subvert her, and whatever attempts that came up, she could handle with the help of her mate. Finn noted to his brother that if they didn't let her meet anyone, they would guard her indefinitely, a prospect none of them were fond of. Dylan conceded, keeping his reservations silent, but Finn knew even if he was being dazzled, his brother was not—and that was important. As long as they were not both overtaken by the intrigues of another elemental, they could collectively keep Alma safe.

However, Alma's growing power, the possibility of another freak weather occurrence, and Finn's certainty that she was experiencing lust easily as strong as his, kept him on his toes, despite Dolores's distractions. Finn wondered again if he should talk to his charge about the side effect. He had watched her reaction when she had received a letter from her grandmother that made her blush and wondered if it was a warning of the symptoms. When he picked it up later while Alma was with Dylan running errands, he found two pages scrawled in a language he couldn't begin to interpret. He didn't know for sure that the letter was about the full power side effect of lust, but he didn't know that it wasn't. He knew her grandmother would have every reason for cautioning Alma. The idea of discussing something so intimate was intimidating. Finn himself didn't even want to think about lust in conjunction with his charge, much less talk to her about it. He reassured himself as he tossed and turned in bed, waiting for another windstorm or a scream to puncture the night's stillness that she would talk to him about it if she needed to. He knew she would more likely talk to Dylan about it, and Dylan would bring it to his attention. He told himself, directing his thoughts back on the beautiful and enigmatic Dolores, he was there to protect Alma and he wouldn't let himself get any more involved than he had to.

thirteen

Dylan was awake when the sound of the wind swiftly rising signified that Alma was going through another surge of the elemental power transforming her body. He scrambled out of bed, taking the stairs at a run; Alma wasn't screaming this time, thank goodness, but the sudden sharp rise in the local wind speed was definitely not something that should be allowed to continue. The experiences he had seen his brother go through, that Alma was going through, dulled anticipation of his own future experience coming into his full abilities. He knew the process would be, at the very least, painful and he would find himself and his power out of control. The "power surges" as Finn and Alma had termed them were unpleasant judging from Alma's screams the first time it had happened to her.

Dylan entered Alma's bedroom behind Finn. He wondered, as he had multiple times before, whether it would have been a better idea for him to take the room next to Alma's instead. While they had flipped a coin in the interest of fairness, Dylan knew his brother annoyed and frustrated Alma and that the enigmatic, flighty woman had the same effect on his brother. He recalled his father telling him when he was young he seemed suited for the role of "peacekeeper" in any situation. It was a designation that would cement his partnership with his hot-tempered, impulsive brother. They had other siblings, but the two—Dylan and Finn—were the best suited to protect other elementals, to act as bodyguards or negotiators in tense situations. Dylan, with his easygoing nature and readily soothing manner was the model diplomat, while Finn never hesitated to put his life in danger to meet his goals.

Finn, perhaps remembering he had made matters worse the previous time that Alma had been in this state, hesitated next to her bed, looking down at her. She wasn't screaming. She wasn't even awake. But the wind intensifying outside rattled the windows. It was enough to tell both Dylan and Finn something was amiss. Even if they had been deaf, the way Alma was moving, writhing in the bed, in her sleep, was evidence enough. Dylan was relieved on his brother's behalf that it seemed Alma had worn pajamas to bed this time. Her nudity hadn't bothered him—other than confirming that Alma was undeniably a beautiful woman even without clothing, something he had suspected anyway. Dylan had conceded that a relationship with Alma and he wouldn't work out; he couldn't give her the demanding, challenging pressure she needed from a mate.

The two stood and stared at Alma for a long moment, neither sure what to do. The previous time she had experienced a power surge, she had been awake by the time they had caught on. The wind speed rose sharply. Dylan cringed at how the windows in Alma's room rattled in their frames, the high-pitched wail of the wind moving through nooks and crannies of the building itself. He looked at his brother in concern, and felt himself blushing slightly as Alma let out a low, throaty moan. It was obvious that she was in the throes of a vivid and apparently erotic dream, her senses cranked to the hilt. Finn touched Alma, and Dylan knocked his hand away. Dylan had contacted Alma's grandmother after the first power surge and mentioned the lightning that had accompanied it. *"Was Finn in contact with her when it happened?"* Lorene had asked sharply. *"Lightning is the manifestation of air and fire combined. They're both unstable elementals, their powers came together. It's dangerous—try to make sure it doesn't happen again."* He hadn't told his brother, and Dylan was still digesting the importance of what Alma's grandmother had said, but he understood the warning.

Just as Dylan knocked aside Finn's attempt to awaken Alma, the wind shifted, becoming more violent. Dylan and Finn jumped, startled when the windows rattled harder, the sound of the wind shaking the panes of glass. Before either of them could organize another thought, the glass shattered, the fragments being sucked out into the night. Wind surged through the room, scattering loose paper and knocking heavier items around. Dylan knew he had to act. Alma wasn't going to wake soon, at least not before her abilities made more of a mess than could be easily explained by freak weather.

Dylan placed his hands firmly on her shoulders, pinning her down to the mattress as he focused all of his thoughts on the spell he had used before. He murmured the spell, feeling the cold, calm pressure of his water energy flowing through his body. He repeated the incantation again and again, calling upon his ability to dampen and suppress the flow of energy rocking Alma.

He sent waves of calming energy through Alma's body until the squall gradually died down. The howling, keening, and wailing wind faltered. Alma shivered. Dylan felt the power coursing through her body tingling through his touch. He let go of her as the wind calmed to a draft.

"Alma," Dylan spoke softly. "Alma." He kept his voice above a whisper, but he wanted to wake her.

Finn stared at the broken window, then glanced from it to the woman he had sworn to protect. Absorbing the shock of the broken window, he moved between Dylan and Alma and gave the woman an abrupt shake. "Wake up!"

Dylan rolled his eyes at his brother's methods—but they were effective. Alma gasped, her dark eyes flying open. She squinted at the men hovering over her and rubbed at her face, shaking her head in confusion.

"What's going on?" she asked, her voice sleepy and plaintive. Dylan smiled slightly. He could tell from the residual flush across her face and chest that her power surge had been precipitated by the same dream-based eroticism that had accompanied his brother's experiences in the destruction of bedroom furniture less than a year before.

"You broke your window," Finn said bluntly, gesturing to the empty frame.

Alma sat up alert, startled by the accusation, looking in the direction Finn was pointing. Dylan sat on the edge of her bed shaking his head. While his brother had many sterling qualities, dealing with crises that didn't call for either beating someone up or destroying property was not one of them. Alma took in the sight of her broken window for a moment and then turned in confusion to Dylan.

"What? How did I break it? I was asleep…dreaming—"

She blushed a deep crimson. Dylan didn't need intuition to know she was remembering the contents of the dream.

"You damned near created a tornado around the building," Finn said, throwing himself down at the foot of her bed. He smirked. "Sounded like a good dream you were having. Let me guess: Alex?"

Dylan forestalled an angry, embarrassed retort from Alma by picking up a stray stuffed animal that had fallen off of a display shelf in her room and throwing it at his brother. "It doesn't matter what she was dreaming about," Dylan said firmly. "You were having another power surge. The wind grew strong enough to shatter the window. I think most of the shards flew out, but be careful walking around." He gave her a little smile. "We can get someone in to fix the window. How are you feeling?"

Alma was shivering but seemed unaware of it. Dylan wondered if he had gone too far in correcting the flow of energy running through her body, countering it with the weight and calm of his own.

"I feel cold…and like I shoved a fork into an electrical socket."

Dylan chuckled, knowing the description was probably an apt one. Only a few days out from her birthday, when she would assume her full powers, Alma was expected to experience a great deal of power. Electricity was an odd manifestation for air-based elemental sensations, but Dylan knew from his studies it wasn't impossible.

"I might have overdone it a bit with the spell," Dylan admitted. "It was pretty intense. Do you think you'll be able to go back to sleep? Or would you rather not with the broken window?"

There were security concerns to be considered; while a window wasn't a huge barrier to entry, the lack of one created a vulnerability if someone was watching the house. It would be stupid of Dylan and Finn to be there to defend Alma against other elementals, only to have her fall prey to a regular human burglar.

"I can sleep on the couch. Might be better." Alma continued to shiver, pulling the blankets around her more tightly. Dylan was concerned; he glanced at Finn, on the point of asking his brother to use his magic to correct his overzealous use of power to calm her.

"Just make sure you don't wreck the windows downstairs too," Finn suggested with a little grin. Alma scowled at him, for a moment looking hurt, then stuck her tongue out at Finn.

"At least a window isn't as embarrassing to replace as a bed," she retorted. "I think I'm going to make myself a hot chocolate before I go back to sleep. Would you like one, Dylan?"

Dylan grinned, knowing it was Alma's intent to snub his older brother, and agreeing with her both in principle and practice.

"I'd love one." Dylan stood, gesturing for Alma to precede him out of the room.

She climbed out of bed, deliberately avoiding Finn as she pulled on a thick bathrobe and padded out of her bedroom. Finn shrugged, but Dylan knew that he was frustrated with himself. He couldn't be angry at the snub—he had earned it—but he couldn't not feel slighted. While Finn wasn't the most thoughtful of people, or the most introspective, Dylan knew his older brother wasn't unintelligent.

"You know, big bro," Dylan said with a little grin. "Considering the lust you have, and how much charm you have with the women, you are really, really striking out with Alma. Maybe you should think about why that is." Dylan left his brother to contemplate in silence.

He was certain he knew something neither Alma nor Finn could see; that if they would get past the barrier of their tumultuous tendencies, they would actually be good for each other. It was odd for him to realize that he was the "mature adult" of the three. He understood where Alma was coming from—she loved her freedom and was too self-determined to comfortably settle for an arranged marriage, or for a relationship that didn't stimulate her.

Dylan was surprised at how well he got along with her. Although he had a diplomatic tendency, he'd found most air elementals to be all style and no substance, to be flashy and charming but ultimately very shallow and often annoying. While Alma wasn't without flaws, he admired that she put work into becoming a respected translator and that she had ambition and motivation as well as enough discipline to back it up. She was flighty in her personal life and in her emotions, but from a professional standpoint, she was a different creature.

Dylan watched Alma move around the kitchen with absentminded grace, reaching without looking for items she needed. He smiled to himself, noticing she preferred to make her hot chocolate from scratch—which didn't align with what he thought he knew of her speed-oriented personality. She took out a small saucepan and rummaged for items she needed in the pantry: unsweetened cocoa, sugar, salt, vanilla extract, and milk from the fridge. Dylan appreciated Alma's culinary skills; he had a basic ability to cook, and his brother Finn made dishes without burning them, though he still occasionally mixed-up salt and sugar, which didn't always bode well for coffee. Alma had spent enough time with her grandmother, growing up steeped in a family that loved food; she was both proficient and comfortable in a kitchen. In some ways, Dylan thought Alma was contradictory; he had seen her settle for peanut butter on saltine crackers for lunch in the midst of work, bringing the food to her mouth and eating it without tasting it; he had seen her devour the worst greasy spoon hamburgers he had ever eaten while they were traveling; but certain things—like hot chocolate—seemed to have an importance to her.

She looked up from stirring, feeling his gaze on her. "Grandma taught me this back before I could even see over the stove. I've tweaked the recipe slightly."

Dylan saw what she meant by a "tweak" when Alma added a healthy amount of whiskey to each mug of hot chocolate, handing one to him with a grin. Dylan sipped the thick, rich drink, able to both smell and taste the whiskey, but not too strongly. He suggested they sit outside to talk. He didn't know what decision his brother had come to regarding Alma's snub, but he knew she would want privacy to talk. They stepped onto the patio that connected to the living room, and Alma took her favored chair while Dylan took the other. He waited for Alma to decide what it was she wanted to talk about.

"So, Finn wasn't that far off, actually," she said, glancing down into her mug.

Dylan smiled faintly to himself.

"I was having an erotic dream when the power surge happened, but it wasn't Alex. At least, I don't think it was. I couldn't see the person's face clearly in the dream. We were in the middle of some kind of fight—not exactly with each other, although we were bickering between dealing with other people—and then the fight was over, and we were alone."

Dylan watched Alma's face redden with a blush.

"Of course, our bickering turned into something else, and right about the time you woke me up, it was at the best part." She sipped her whiskey-enhanced hot chocolate.

Dylan felt her working to consciously suppress her feelings of embarrassment. "From everything I know, intense lust and eroticism is not unusual when you're coming into the last part of the transition," Dylan pointed out. "Some people suggest that if you haven't already found your mate by that time, you get some indications of who they might be." He didn't tell her that Finn had experienced similar dreams with a similarly mysterious woman. He didn't know for sure that there was anything to it.

"You know," Alma said softly, sitting back in her chair and looking across at Dylan with a little smile. "My life would be so much easier if we were attracted to each other."

Dylan chuckled. "I think all of our lives would be easier if you and I were attracted to each other," Dylan commented. "Your grandmother would get off your back, you'd be able to do what you wanted, and we could just wait for me to reach my elemental peak next year and be set." Dylan shrugged. "I'll try to work on becoming attracted to you, if you'll work on getting the hots for me," he joked.

Alma laughed and Dylan raised his mug to her.

"In seriousness, though," Alma said, after she had clinked her mug against his, her smile dissolving into a more solemn expression. "What do you think about Finn and me meeting the two cousins?"

Dylan hesitated. He was still uncertain about the situation. While he could appreciate both Finn and Alma having needs, and that Alma's life had been essentially turned upside down—her social life suppressed by the danger incumbent upon her development into a full elemental—there was something about Alex and Dolores that rang a quiet alarm in his mind. He had been on the forums before and spoken with several members—learning tricks from water elementals, getting to know earth elementals and their strange ways, getting information from air elementals, and obtaining tech rumors from fire elementals. It wasn't normal for a member of the site to take a sudden intense interest in a newbie the way Alex seemed to have taken in Alma. While she had been discreet, and Dylan knew he could trust her to do so, there had been some verification of her lineage as part of the signup process. There was no way to be sure how many people knew she was not only an air elemental, but that she was a staggeringly powerful one whose grandmother was possibly the strongest water elemental living.

"I think you should be careful," Dylan said slowly. "I mean, obviously Finn and I can't cover you in bubble wrap and expect you to ever find a mate. That'd be pretty conspicuous, and I'm not sure you could pull off the look." He grinned. "But from my experience, it seems strange someone would be so interested in a newcomer so quickly."

Alma nodded, looking thoughtful.

Dylan continued. "I wouldn't be against your meeting them just generally, but you should both be prepared if something happens."

Alma glanced down at her mug. "I'm kind of between a rock and a hard place," she said wryly. "I need a mate to keep people from trying to force me into marriage or kill me, but I have to deal with those very people in order to find a mate to protect me from them." She laughed, the sound slightly bitter. "I just wish I could have been a run-of-the-mill elemental, nothing too extraordinary—like my cousins. Not a one of them has this problem."

Dylan shrugged. "Yeah, but not one of them can knock out a window with a sex dream either, I bet."

"Good point." Alma blushed a deep red, but she was chuckling. "I think I might finally warm up! Ahh, the powers of hot chocolate and alcohol."

Dylan shared her grin, but he couldn't quite shake his sense of unease about the planned meeting the next day, even though he knew without concrete evidence, it wouldn't make sense to openly oppose it.

fourteen

Alma woke up with the tremors still dancing up and down her arms and legs, the lingering evidence of her late-night power surge reminding her she'd come into complete possession of her abilities as an elemental in less than twenty-four hours. In some ways, she was excited—in others she was filled with dread. She knew her entire training as a child had been aimed at making sure she maintained control when she became a full elemental. But the power surges she had experienced were a portent that made Alma uncertain of how much she could realistically control herself once the full elemental power came into her. She wanted to be out drinking and having fun the eve of her birthday, because on the day of, she had no idea what she would be like.

On the forum, she had read some stories elementals told about their final transition. While most laughed off the power surges and other symptoms, Alma thought there were some situations she wouldn't know how to handle. What if she developed a fever? Or went into a coma? Those things could happen. What if the power overwhelmed her, and she utterly could not control it?

At the back of her mind, in the part not occupied with worries about the possibility of a near-death experience during her transition, her lustful urges were spiking. While she had found Dylan and Finn attractive enough since she had known them, it hadn't been too difficult to be around them. That changed after she woke up on the living room couch. Only hours after her conversation with Dylan, where she had joked that her life would be so much easier if only, they were attracted to each other, those words came back to haunt her. As she tried to work on an assignment, one of the last two she needed to complete, she found herself uncharacteristically hot and cold all over, distracted by Dylan walking across the living room to the kitchen, and again by Finn in only a pair of pajama pants. Normally she was not even inclined to notice what her houseguest-bodyguards were wearing or not wearing, but the slight indentation of Finn's hip above his drawstring pants was more than enough to send Alma into an arousal so intense she bit her lip to keep from speaking.

She avoided looking at them, reminding herself she would see Alex in a few hours and that he was a much more acceptable target for her lust. But it was impossible to ignore Dylan when he asked her a question in a soft voice, or to avoid the rush of sensation she felt at the brush of Finn's fingers against her skin when he handed her a mug of coffee. She pulled up a picture that Alex had sent her and focused on the air elemental; he was as intensely attractive as before, but somehow didn't inspire the same immediate need Alma felt around Finn and Dylan. Her mind was playing tricks on her; she wanted nothing more than to get her work completed and meet with Alex and his cousin.

Instead, her mind kept leading her on tangents, providing oh so helpful images of what it would be like to see Dylan naked, to be wrapped tightly in Finn's arms while he touched her everywhere. She tried working isolated from the two men on her patio and then in her bedroom. But even without their presence, her imagination was in overdrive, more than happy to supply her with fantasies that made translating from Russian into Mandarin an impossibility. Alma decided that she would just have an unproductive day, and that she might as well take advantage of the opportunity to spend as much time as she wanted getting ready for her meeting with Alex.

She realized her delusion in the shower when the hot water run out and was replaced by a frigid spray. She had intended to get herself clean and then primp, so she would look her best. Instead, as the hot water coursed over her body, she had found it impossible not to run her hands all over herself, let them linger where her fingertips would do the best, and watch the revolving door of potential lovers in her mind—Dylan, Finn, Alex, men she barely remembered from earlier dalliances, characters from TV. The cold water jolted her from her sensual reverie. Alma clamped down on her lust filled thoughts, taking a deep breath and stepping out of the shower, determined to finish getting ready and be on her way. She focused on her makeup and hair before she faced a quandary: what to wear? It was a casual lunch, nothing fancy, but Alma's stomach roiled with impatient uncertainty as she looked through her closet and drawers, picking up an item and then casting it aside just as quickly.

After four changes of clothes, she finally felt like she had struck the proper balance: a skirt that fell to midthigh in softly pleated black cotton, paired with a T-shirt from a band she loved, a light jacket, and a pair of ankle boots. It wasn't too fancy, she thought looking at herself in the mirror, but it showed off her best assets without overemphasizing them. She slipped on a bracelet and necklace and heard a knock at her bedroom door.

"Aren't you ready yet?" Finn called through.

Alma grabbed the earrings that went with her necklace and rushed to the door, opening it to admit Finn while she brought the first of the pair of earrings up to her ear to fasten it.

Finn let out a low, appreciative whistle at her ensemble. "Why didn't you dress up like this to meet me?" he asked with a wolfish grin.

Alma rolled her eyes. "In case you don't recall, I didn't meet you willingly." She fastened the other earring and looked at Finn; he had taken the same approach she had—fitted jeans, a pair of comfortable but well-maintained shoes, and a button-down shirt in a deep red that contrasted his bright eyes. "That's a subtle piece of psychology," she said, pointing to his shirt, "matching your clothes to Dolores's hair." She gave him a smirk, throwing a lip color into her purse along with her powder compact. She hadn't gone overboard with the makeup, just enough to enhance her bone structure and give her eyes depth—certainly not what she would wear the next night to go out.

Finn rolled his eyes at her. "Let's hit the road. You don't want to be late to meet your mate, do you?"

Alma scowled at the sarcasm in Finn's voice. "I am NOT meeting my mate. I'm meeting…a very interesting and charming elemental who I might want to have sex with sometime."

Finn snorted at her characterization, gesturing for Alma to precede him down the stairs. She had chosen a soft, slightly floral perfume; an old-fashioned scent she had long ago decided was perfect for such occasions.

Dylan was waiting downstairs, dressed casually in jeans and a T-shirt, and he echoed his brother's commendation. "Just so you know," he told her with a grin, "if Alex is too much of an idiot to sweep you off your feet, it won't take much to convince me."

Alma blushed slightly, biting her bottom lip. "I will keep that in mind," she said, giving him a flirty smile.

Finn brushed past her, making every inch of her skin feel electrified, heading for the door.

"Come on, guys. We're going to be late."

Alma's anxiety mounted as they arrived at the café where she and Finn planned to meet Dolores and Alex. She felt her hands shaking, echoing the vibration she felt moving through her bones—an intensely electric feeling she knew was the power working its way through her, changing her. She fidgeted in the passenger seat, wondering how she had somehow been convinced to let Finn drive. As she shifted around, feeling an almost itching sensation, she thought it was for the best. Dylan followed behind in the car he and Finn had bought during the time they were staying with her. Dylan intended to hang out and wait for the meeting to be over, to make sure they were safe. He and Finn had also equipped Alma with one of the contact buttons they each had. Failing that, Dylan's water-aligned intuition would enable him to track them.

Alma couldn't imagine Alex and Dolores would go to such an extreme as kidnapping or attacking them in public. It would be bad for elementals as a whole, and they'd face a dire punishment—potentially even death—if they attempted such. She considered that she hadn't thought she would be abducted, or that one of her clients would have allowed her abductors near her. She understood the need to be cautious, but as power buzzed through her veins and along her nerves, she couldn't help feeling as though she could handle anything Alex or Dolores could throw at her and Finn. She also couldn't help entertaining lust-filled thoughts about the man she had been talking to, her mind rejecting the possibility he might attack her. At least, she thought, if he was unsafe—if he had ulterior motives—his air alignment would ensure that he wouldn't move directly. It would be something sneakier. She reminded herself, charmed as she was by him, she had to remember he well could be her enemy.

In spite of Finn's moans about the possibility of being late, they were the first to arrive. They took a table. Alma rolled her eyes at Finn's scoff when the waiter suggested they were there together on a date.

"Just friends, waiting for our dates, actually," she said, giving the man a bright, charming smile. The lust, coiled tightly inside of her, hadn't failed to notice the waiter was attractive; tall and lean, with dark eyes and collar length black hair, he visibly warmed to her attention. He took their drink orders and lingered, exchanging pleasantries with Alma until Finn brusquely reminded him there were other tables that needed his attention. Alma shifted and squirmed in her seat, feeling the heat in her body banking and rising, her eyes scanning the crowd of pedestrians beyond the outside terrace for any sign of Alex or Dolores. *What if they stand us up?* She bit her lip and then checked to make sure she hadn't marred her makeup. She told herself firmly the two cousins wouldn't; they were just as interested in meeting as she and Finn were.

Just when Alma's anxiety was reaching fever pitch, she spotted Dolores's brilliant red hair and shifted her gaze to find Alex standing next to her, speaking with the hostess. The woman at the desk smiled at the two charming elementals and gestured for them to follow her.

"They're here," Alma told Finn, whose back was to the hostess. She fought the urge to stand, sitting on her hands as she impatiently waited for them to make their way to the table. Words were pressing at the front of her mind, crowding her lips, and she took a deep breath to push down the excitement she felt. As they approached the table, Alma noticed Alex was even more attractive than his pictures; his dark hair was mussed, his bright eyes a deeper, almost blueberry shade, and a ready smile curving his lips. He wore a pair of jeans that looked as though they had seen better days and barely clung to his lean hips, giving Alma the impression she could easily pull them off of him. With the jeans he wore a black T-shirt with text she couldn't quite read, too distracted in her gaze to focus. Over the tee, he wore a red jacket with a gray scarf topping it off. A deep tingle swept through her at the sight of him, and blood rushed to her face when his gaze fell on her, his smile deepening.

She stood, more to give herself something to do, an outlet for the excess energy she felt, than a conscious gesture of manners. Alex approached her quickly, leaning in to kiss her on the cheek and give her a friendly hug. He smelled of cloves and something pleasingly woody and green, mingled with a faint cigarette smoke smell that Alma had to admit was alluring. Dolores had been claimed by Finn, who was hugging her tightly, but Alma barely noticed as she and Finn switched; her mind was still full of Alex as she embraced Dolores, pressing her cheek against the other woman's.

"It's so good to finally meet you," Dolores said, her low,

sultry voice softened further by her accent. She and Alex took their seats next to their respective dates, and Alma felt her heart fluttering, her throat going dry. Her head was spinning, unable to process what was happening.

"My God, Alma, you should have warned me," Alex commented lowly, giving Alma a not-quite-lewd look from head to toe. "You must be used to her," he said to Finn, "after knowing her so long. But I can't seem to take my eyes off of her."

Finn nodded absently, looking at Dolores with definite attraction in his eyes, smiling a faintly drunken grin. Alma felt a moment of jealousy at the other woman's obvious beauty and the way Finn was responding to it—it helped her to get over her momentary shock of absolute attraction to Alex.

"Sure you can take your eyes off me," she said with a slight drawl. "I wouldn't want you to strain yourself."

Alex laughed, and Alma felt the warm glow of his charm once more. The waiter approached and was immediately bowled over by the charged atmosphere; Alma could feel the power inside of her swelling, and the wind around them picked up. She suppressed it, carefully focusing her intentions. She had never been around two powerful air elementals simultaneously—it was like light shining on a deprived plant, the first warm rays of sunlight through snow. She felt the cousins' energy pushing through the deep block Dylan had put on her to help her get through the power surge. The spell was fading away, eroded by the high energy the two cousins brought with them.

"I've been told I should avoid southern girls, you know," Alex commented after the waiter left, taking their drink orders in a daze. "Dolores's brother kindly informed me you're all wild heathens who rip good English boys to shreds."

Alma laughed, almost gasping as Alex's hand came to rest on her knee. He didn't move it upward, which would have immediately alerted Alma, but casually left it where it was, the warmth of his skin sinking into hers.

"We get such a bad reputation. I happen to think it's good for English boys to court southern girls. You guys need some loosening up." Dolores was asking Finn about his life, about how he had come to be friends with Alma's family. Finn, almost visibly responding to the energy around him, his blue eyes flickering with a light Alma both admired and resented, explained their grandmothers knew each other. He was close to admitting he was protection—a bodyguard—when Alma kicked him underneath the table, using the leg that Alex's hand hadn't claimed. He came out of his reverie, coughing and saying he and Alma had met as children, and they were roommates out of convenience.

Conversation ebbed and flowed. Alma had to keep a tight grip on her abilities as the lunch progressed; she considered that she should have consulted her grandmother before agreeing to the date. It was clear to her Alex and Dolores were both potent elementals in their own right, radiating charm and playful intelligence, inciting a lively debate about authors and music. Alma felt her power growing in the presence of the two elementals, and it became increasingly difficult to keep her power under control. It bubbled, flowed, and surged through her. In spite of her intense attraction to Alex, she could see the two cousins were probing for information. She maintained the conversation but wondered whether they were gathering intelligence for someone who might have less than friendly intentions towards her. She felt her mind picking up pace, her thoughts gaining speed to a point she almost felt as though she were on a potent stimulant. She asked for another drink to suppress it, almost trembling with the excess of energy she was experiencing.

Dolores was clearly feeding into Finn's fiery energy, using the powers at her disposal to charm and pique. Alma found herself momentarily distracted time and again, almost resenting Finn's ready response to the woman. She was torn away from her disgust each time by Alex, with no trace of confusion or irritation.

"You mentioned traveling," he said, calling her attention back to him. Alma noticed absently that his hand had shifted on her knee, and he was kneading and caressing it slightly—though he kept his touch respectful, not trying to work his way up her thigh. "Where all have you been?"

Alma plunged into a discussion of different parts of the world and found that, while Alex picked up languages quickly, he was not the linguistic savant she was. He praised her ready translations of random phrases into a variety of languages, countering with the handful he knew, and soon they were exchanging flirtatious pleasantries in esoteric languages, Alex's comments becoming more and more suggestive at each turn.

Alma lost track of time completely. They were enjoying coffee and dessert, Dolores prodding and cajoling Finn into sampling her fruit and zabaglione, when Alma finally had enough presence of mind to realize they had been enjoying each other's company for more than an hour. "Shit! Finn, we have that appointment we have to get to."

Finn gave her a confused look, clearly reluctant to end his conversation with Dolores.

"Remember? Dylan was going to meet us at the office?"

The mention of his brother's name sobered Finn, and he

nodded quickly, his eyes losing some of the fire Dolores's stoking had inspired.

"That is such a shame!" Alex said, his hand tightening playfully on her knee. Alma looked at him, blushing slightly at the intent gaze he turned on her. "It must be an important meeting for you to disrupt such a good time," his voice softened. "If it's not important, you could reschedule." There was something in Alex's manner, the compelling look in his eyes that made Alma briefly dizzy. She was on the point of agreeing with him—after all, Dylan could wait a little longer—when some native instinct stopped her short. She felt a slight shudder work through her body, and she gave him a regret-filled smile.

"I'm afraid it's very important," she replied, letting her voice take on a rueful tone. "Legal things, you understand. I'm on the lawyer's time—he won't reschedule." She gave Finn another undetectable kick to the shins beneath the table to prevent his protest. "As it is, I suspect we've kept him waiting already." She gave Alex a charming smile. She felt something stirring inside of her—not lust, but a cunning, a kind of inarticulate knowledge of her own power. "I'm sure you can understand." The words left her lips without conscious thought, and she felt something inside of her pushing outward, a persuasiveness she had never known she had. Alex looked briefly confused, but then nodded slowly.

"I understand. It's a shame, but I'll have to hope we can see both of you again soon."

Alma felt odd and gave herself a little shake. The waiter brought the bill, and Alex would hear nothing of either her or Finn contributing to the total. He insisted on paying for the entire bill and tip. Alma gave in, smiling to herself despite the strange feelings. She felt herself smiling as Alex handed her a scrap of receipt with his phone number on the back. She let him walk her to the car, feeling a little outside of herself. Something was different in that moment she had persuaded Alex, some ability she had never used before. She saw Dolores chatting with Finn as she accompanied him to the car, and Alma stopped at the passenger side, at a loss for what to do.

Alex leaned in and gave her a hungry kiss. Alma's confusion and introspection dissolved, her lust spiked as he rested his hands on her waist, holding her tightly but respectfully. She let out a soft moan as Alex deepened the kiss, nipping at her bottom lip playfully. In that moment she would have gladly remained there indefinitely, overwhelmed by the sweetness of Alex's tongue and the way his body vibrated against hers, taut with energy and desire. She lost ability to even care what happened next or that Dylan was still waiting for the all-clear, as Alex pressed her against the door of the car. He moaned softly against her lips, his grip on her waist tightening. Alma melted against him, swept up in his attractiveness and the steady pulse of lust in her veins. Her mind consumed with need, her body kindled with desire, she felt her hands trembling and her heart pounding. She would have let him do anything to her without complaint, but Alex remained moderately respectful, more mindful of the public venue than Alma. She was on the verge of moving further to increase the tension between them when she was interrupted by a chirp from her phone.

The sound divided the thick fog consuming Alma, and she broke away from the kiss, gasping and panting for breath. She hadn't experienced anything so intense since kissing Finn. Alma pushed the thought down, shaking her head and reaching for her phone. "That's Dylan," she called to Finn, who was kissing Dolores with similar fervor Alma had experienced a moment before. "We need to get going, Andy." She used the nickname to break through the almost palpable haze of desire surrounding the other two; she knew Finn hated it. He broke away from Dolores, confused for a moment before realization set in.

"Right! Yes. I'm so sorry, Dolly," he murmured to the other woman, giving her a brief kiss before breaking away. "We'll get together again soon."

The two cousins seemed disappointed, but Alex gave Alma a last, lingering glance full of promise and desire before she got into the passenger seat.

"Are you okay to drive?" Alma asked Finn tartly as she fastened her seat belt.

Finn rolled his eyes. "You had more to drink than I did." He started the car and sent Dylan a text advising that they were clear. Alma stared out the window and tried to conquer her tense desire, telling herself that since she had Alex's phone number, she could see him again whenever she wanted. She added his number to her contacts, thinking of inviting him to her birthday.

As they drove back to the apartment, Alma's intense lustful sensations and almost brutal power ebbed, and she turned her thoughts to the less than normal events of the lunch. She remembered Alex's persuasive comment suggesting she reschedule and how she had almost submitted and given in to his will before something deep inside of her rebelled. She had turned the same tactic—whatever it was—back on him. Reviewing the events of the meeting without the rose-colored glasses of intense attraction, Alma knew something was going on with Dolores and Alex.

"Did anything about that lunch seem odd to you?" she asked Finn, shifting in her seat.

Finn glanced at her skeptically, shrugging. "Not really," he said quickly.

Alma raised an eyebrow, wondering how much charm Dolores had been radiating at the fire elemental while Alma had been distracted by Alex's overtures.

Finn started to say something, then hesitated. "There was something a little strange about it, now that you mention it." He made a turn, his brow furrowing. "It was like they didn't want us to leave their presence."

Alma nodded slowly. "They were determined to keep us talking to them, to keep our attention on each of them." Alma licked her lips. She was more than willing at the time to give Alex all of her attention, the part of her mind reeling with lust and power had taken over. "Whenever we tried to talk to each other, one or the other of them would interrupt and reel us back in."

Finn nodded. "What do you think?" he asked her, for once deferring to her opinion.

Alma shrugged. "It could be nothing. It could be that...." She bit her bottom lip in thought. "They're air elementals. We're all very good at intelligence gathering. They could be spies."

Finn snorted. "Well, whoever hired them made a mistake, then. You are a better counterintelligence agent than they are spies. Thanks for kicking me—I think my legs will be black and blue for a week, though."

Alma grinned. "You were about to give us away! You're like...a highly less-effective James Bond. Jeez."

"Hey! I could be every bit as effective as James Bond. I could seduce Dolores and discover what's going on." Finn scowled. Alma rolled her eyes, laughing again. "You were calling her Dolly. She had you wrapped around her little finger, Andy."

Finn's scowl deepened. "She did not! She's just...a very charming and attractive woman. Now that I know, I can totally keep out of her clutches."

Alma shook her head in disbelief. She had to admit, despite her suspicions about Alex, she barely restrained herself from sending him a text message and continuing their flirtation. She would talk to Dylan first, but she had almost concluded that, spy or not, she wanted Alex at her birthday party. He was too flattering, too deliciously attractive, and too attentive for her to forego his presence, even if it was not the best idea to invite a potential spy to witness a moment that could be vulnerable for her.

fifteen

Alma could tell Dylan was disturbed by the possible reason for Alex's and Dolores's interest in her and Finn. "We kept to the story," she told him quietly, sipping at a beer in the late afternoon light of the balcony. "But I think they were trying to shake it up, trying to get us to admit the truth."

He nodded slowly, accepting her theory. "The key would be to discover who they're working for, then," he said matter-of-factly, taking a sip of his own beer.

Alma shrugged. "You and Finn are the investigators. I'm just a lowly translator."

Dylan rolled his eyes. "We'd put you on the payroll if we could. Between your language skills and the presence of mind you showed at lunch earlier...."

She had told him about the strange moments that had passed, where she had felt Alex's will pressing against hers, and had returned the courtesy. Dylan pointed out that air elementals had their own kind of intuition and their own psychic strengths. While water elementals in full possession of their abilities could "read" other people to an uncanny degree, air elementals tended towards projecting their thoughts and wishes onto others. It was a magic Alma's grandmother hadn't introduced her to, but which made sense. She had always been proud of her persuasion skills, and persuasiveness was definitely an air-aligned trait, but she had never felt something as direct as what she had experienced with Alex.

"The thing is, I'm kind of going crazy," Alma admitted. She felt as though she had an itch she couldn't scratch, some tingle she couldn't reach on her own. Something was driving her to maintain the connection with Alex. "Even knowing he could be a spy, I want him at my birthday party."

Dylan nodded slowly, thinking about what she had said. "I think, if you can keep your keen sense of survival, it might not be a bad idea."

Alma was surprised by Dylan's statement.

"I mean, we're not going to find out what they're after unless you interact with them more. You'll be vulnerable, but you'll have Finn and me both there with you...and your friends."

Alma bit her lip, thinking of the way Alex had kissed her, the absolute charm he radiated. She was in danger of becoming attached to him, beyond a casual attraction.

"Besides, when you come into your full powers, I doubt he'd be able to stand up against you."

Alma chuckled. "He's an air elemental too. And not a wimpy one, either."

Dylan shook his head. "You're underestimating yourself. You were able to keep yourself under control at lunch. You said yourself you kept getting hunches, kept pulling away from his charm."

Alma sighed. "Yes, but my...uh...ah, to hell with it. I'm

getting more and more turned on by the hour, and he's so gorgeous."

Dylan laughed out loud, rolling his eyes. "If you really need help restraining yourself, you can count on me to wet blanket you."

Alma snorted at the turn of phrase, thinking it was a good description of the spell he had cast to suppress the violence of her powers and the sensation of Dylan infusing his more stable, watery energy into her.

"If you don't think it will be a total disaster and get me killed...," she said, trailing off.

Dylan shook his head. "You can handle this."

Alma pulled her cell phone out of her pocket, feeling palpable relief. Maybe she was wrong; maybe Alex and Dolores weren't spies. She texted him a flirtatious note, adding that she would enjoy having his help in celebrating her birthday. If Dylan believed in her ability to take care of herself in that fraught time, she would have to believe in herself.

Alex texted back he had hoped she'd want to see him again so soon. Alma gave Dylan a little smile, taking her phone with her as she went to her bedroom, beginning a rapid-fire exchange with the other elemental. While she knew she shouldn't trust him, she warmed to his enthusiasm, blushing and feeling as giddy as she had in his presence. She told herself firmly she would have to be careful—she could easily experience another power surge in the night—but it almost seemed worth it.

sixteen

After they came home from the lunch date, the repairman arrived to fix the broken window. Alma hadn't considered how odd it would be to have just one window broken out until he asked what had happened.

"Oh," she said, latching on to the news coverage of another odd windstorm. "It was that windstorm last night. I heard it put out several windows in the area." The repairman nodded, commenting that he had been busy all day with repairs. When Alma heard about the broken windows, she felt guilty. She was still waiting to hear from her grandmother about what a horrible display it was and how she should have controlled herself better. Then she remembered that, while coming into her full powers her grandmother had flooded her childhood home and caused another small, localized flood on another location when she had been consumed with grief at the passing of her first husband. She would understand, Alma thought. The lack of a phone call was likely a signal. Her grandmother knew there was nothing Alma could have done in the situation to prevent the windstorm from happening.

As she continued to text Alex, Alma didn't realize she was forgetting her misgivings about the man; instead she was responding to his air-aligned charm, to the easygoing flattery that even she knew air elementals excelled in. She heard herself giggling at his comments, glanced at her phone every few moments throughout dinner and even afterwards, waiting to see what he would say next. To judge by his preoccupation, Finn was going through a similar situation with Dolores, and when Alma noticed, the sharp stab of jealousy resurfaced. *It's just my superpowered elemental hormones,* she firmly told herself. They'd had another vicious argument when she suggested she was fine with Alex coming to her birthday, but she was hesitant to invite Dolores. Her reasoning was that the woman had nearly charmed Finn into admitting everything, and Finn couldn't keep himself properly on the task of protecting her if Dolores was around to distract him. Dylan had interrupted the argument in his usual diplomatic fashion, telling them both firmly but gently that if either were having a problem keeping the correct caution, he would simply use his spells to bring them back in line. They both conceded.

Alma decided a new outfit was in order for her birthday celebration, and so she spent the rest of her evening scanning local boutiques, wanting to get the shopping done as quickly as possible the next day before she went out. She wanted to look irresistible. The part of her mind not engaged in planning and making sure her friends would be available for her celebration, was dwelling on the air elemental. She pictured him easily in her mind, sprawled in bed with her, his hands wandering over her body as his intense blue eyes looked down at her full of lust. She had not failed to notice his long, deft fingers, the way his touch ignited something inside of her all throughout lunch, bearing the power to distract her from her annoyance at Finn's failure to remember they needed to be cautious. As long as she could avoid revealing too much, she thought, she was not at all adverse to seducing—or being seduced by—the other man.

Alma awoke the morning before her birthday feeling both incredibly, vibrantly alive and on the edge of mania. The sensory overload that had accompanied her first power surge was back, not quite as strong as it was initially, but constant. Even Dylan's magic could not put a dent in the sensation of power running up and down her limbs, coursing through her organs, igniting every part of her. If her attention waivered from controlling her element for even a few moments, the wind rose. She caught Finn and Dylan exchanging a concerned look.

"I'll be okay," she said, irritated at their doubt. Alma put on her most comfortable clothes, choosing fabrics that wouldn't rub against her sensitized skin. In addition to her irritation, she found her lust increasing exponentially. She had to carefully force herself not to look at Finn or Dylan for too long or her mind ran away with fantasies of seducing them, of taking them to her bed and satisfying the insatiable thirst, the itch that was driving her mad. She knew it would be a difficult day—that the next day was unlikely to be much better—but she had to believe she could get through it. She had put so much hope in her plans to go out, had looked forward to it so much that it would have crushed her to back out.

Alex sent a text while she was getting ready to go to the mall with the two brothers, a flirtatious greeting that sent a thrill through her. She knew she had only to make the smallest mention of her desires and Alex would find a way to fulfill them. The same power filling her with knowledge of her own potential, however, also filled her with doubt—suspicion. She considered the quandary; Alex was more than just an elemental who was interested in her. The solution hit her suddenly as she responded to Alex—while she didn't have her grandmother's intuitive insights, her air alignment gave her abilities in divination and her grandmother had taught her extensively as part of her elemental training. She opened the top drawer of her dresser, moving pairs of underwear and bras around until she found the old, worn tarot deck her grandmother had taught her with. Alma heard the wind rising, but she paid little attention. Removing the cards from the pack, she felt the comforting weight of them in her hands, soothing her apprehensions.

Her grandmother had taught her there were always answers to be found. Alma closed her eyes as she shuffled the cards, progressing them through her hands in automatic movements as she moved to sit in the center of her room.

She continued to shuffle until something inside told her to stop. She selected cards, setting them in a spread in front of her with her eyes still closed, relying on muscle memory and divining instinct. While she could divine things from a variety of sources—tea leaves, crystal balls, runes—she was most comfortable with the cards. Alma continued pulling cards until she had a full spread. She then set the rest down next to her. She opened her eyes and studied the cards she had selected, her gaze moving over each one in its position. The swords suit featured prominently. Alma almost rolled her eyes at such an obvious allusion to the situation at hand: swords, being the element of air, were appropriate considering her alignment and Alex's. She took a deeper look, knowing there was more to be seen beyond the obvious. In the position representing herself, she saw the Queen of Swords: the pinnacle of feminine air energy, representing her rise into her final state as a full elemental. It was compromised by the six of swords—a difficult transition, a rite of passage. The three of swords showed the potential for grief, for heartbreak. The outcome was the ace of swords: victory, raw power. The lover's card represented a decision to be made.

Alex's alignment showed itself as the Knight of swords, paired with the Magician. Yet another influence in the spread Alma couldn't quite understand was the World card, representing completion, which gravitated to the Chariot card. Alma shook her head; she would contemplate that influence later. The situation regarding Alex and Alma, and whether or not she should move forward with him, played out with the Tower, followed by the High Priestess in reverse—the need to listen to her instincts. Alma sighed.

She was still contemplating the spread of cards in front of her when a knock sounded at her door. "Come in," she said absently, trying to find out whether she was being told to avoid the situation altogether, or merely being told that she should be cautious. Dylan opened the door and entered, carrying a mug. He took a seat in a chair a few feet away, setting the mug down on Alma's vanity.

"I talked to your grandmother," he said quietly, not wanting to interrupt her contemplation. Alma nodded, thinking of the Tower, the suggestion of a rite of passage, of difficult choices. She looked at the cards advising the potential of grief and heartbreak and wondered if that meant she would be betrayed—that Alex had dark intentions for her, or was working with someone who did. Or that he was simply connected in some way to a potential for betrayal and heartache. She had to decide at some point, the cards were clear on that. But was it the present moment, or some future instance? Alma groaned and scooped up the cards, adding them back to the deck and shuffled it again. She looked up at him, letting her mind drift as she shuffled, looking for clarity.

"She gave me a recipe that should help you with the power surges."

Alma raised an eyebrow.

"It should at least help you function."

Alma nodded. If her grandmother had given Dylan the recipe, she had to trust it would work—at least a little bit. "I'll drink it in a minute."

Dylan watched her for a moment as she finished shuffling and began blindly spreading them. She looked down at the cards, seeing most of the same cards once again. She was too close to the problem. She tried to read deeper into the cards. She understood the choice she would have to make involved not only Alex, but the mysterious third influence, which was fleshed out with the King of Swords in this spread. Alma shook her head and sighed, scooping the cards up and putting them back into the deck, straightening them and putting them back into the case. She bit her bottom lip, deciding she would have to decide for herself; the cards weren't going to give her the answer she sought.

"Let's see that potion," Alma said, standing and putting

the deck away in her underwear drawer once more. She avoided looking too closely at Dylan; just being in his proximity made her feel distracted. He handed her the mug.

"It has chamomile, lemon balm, passionflower, apple, and a little vervain. It'll taste weird, but it should do the trick—infused with water- and earth-aligned ingredients."

Alma nodded, sipping it. It was warm, but not overly hot. It didn't taste as bad as some potions her grandmother had given her over the years; it was slightly sweet, almost a little minty from the lemon balm and vervain. As she drank it in, she felt the power coursing through her recede to a low, constant hum. It wasn't like being normal, but at least it was something she could deal with. Her thoughts slowed, the wind outside abated. Alma finished the drink quickly, grimacing at the lingering sweetness clinging to the back of her throat. It wasn't the worst thing she'd ever drunk, but she would be glad when the need for it was no longer so strong.

"I think you'll need to make that for me again before we go out," Alma said. Although she could feel the magic of the potion working through her, she could already feel the elemental energy transforming her beginning to go to work overwhelming it. Her innate magic did not like to be suppressed and grounded—not when it would be at its peak within twenty-four hours. She took a deep breath. "Okay, let's go to the mall."

seventeen

Alma maintained her self-control while they were shopping, but with great difficulty. She kept her gaze on the ground in front of her, glancing up at the store signs to find the ones she wanted. The potion Dylan had given her had suppressed the power coursing through her body, but it had done little to subdue the lust. In addition to the close proximity of Finn and Dylan, her desire-hazed brain latched on to the good-looking men in close proximity. She was easily distracted, losing her train of thought whenever she spotted someone even slightly attractive, forgetting what store she was looking for. Dylan and Finn tried not to touch her; she was still overly sensitive, her nerves lighting up to every brush of a hand against her arm or shoulder.

Finally, she located the stores she wanted, and Dylan and Finn waited patiently as she moved through the racks indecisively. It was a special birthday and she wanted to look her best, not only because of the occasion, but because she had decided whether or not it was a good idea, she wanted Alex. The tarot cards had been unclear; she knew that she had difficulties ahead, but didn't know what form they would take. Alma was aware of the store clerks watching with amusement as she tried on different dresses, showing them to Dylan and Finn and eliciting their feedback. She knew Finn had lost interest in the exercise quickly, but Dylan was patient, commenting on both the strong points and the weaknesses of each attempted outfit. After half a dozen dresses, Alma pulled the final selection on, zipped it up, and stood before the mirror; compared to some she had tried before, it was almost demure. The skirt fell almost to her knees with satiny folds that flowed from underneath the bust. The plunging neckline and sleeveless top paired with its colors: vivid red with a black bow and black shoulders, was daring enough that Alma felt a rush of sensuality. She slipped on a pair of black patent heels and spun in the confines of the dressing room, giggling with almost girlish delight. The plunging neckline demanded a different bra from the one she wore, and she thought that a pair of stockings would complete the look—but it was perfect.

She stepped out of the dressing room to where Dylan and Finn were waiting for her final attempt. Dylan's eyes widened and he gave Finn a shove to call his attention to Alma's appearance before them. Finn stopped looking around idly, and Alma felt her sense of undirected lust fasten on him as he stared, taking in every inch of her. "Oh my god," he said, his voice barely above a whisper. "You... you could kill a man, looking like that."

Alma blushed, smiling shyly, her heart pounding in her chest. She reminded herself firmly again she had no interest in them, that she was reacting to the desire pulsing a constant dance up and down her veins, to their admiring glances. She licked her lips unconsciously, trying to control her sudden need to pull Finn into one of the dressing rooms and let him rip the dress off of her.

"I think you'll be torturing pretty much every man—and likely women—in that dress. It's perfect," Dylan said, grinning at her.

Alma felt her shy smile spread wider with the warmth of being desired, knowing both of the men were reacting to her physique and the way the dress emphasized each one of her strengths. She almost didn't want to take it off, the feeling was so potent. But she knew walking around the mall, finishing errands, would be difficult in the dress and heels. She retreated into the dressing room, stripping carefully out of the dress and slipping into the clothes she had come into the shop in, taking a few moments to calm herself. It would be soon enough, she thought, her mind turning to Alex.

She got through the last of her purchases—some makeup, the stockings she wanted, and a better bra—just as the potion Dylan had given her was wearing off. "We need to go home," she said lowly. "Now." She was becoming overwhelmed by the feeling of increasing energy in her body, her senses in overdrive, her mind propelled to startling lengths of lightning-fast thought. When they stepped out into the parking garage, she heard the wind picking up, and slid into the back seat of the car, closing her eyes, and focusing all of her mind on controlling the potent power welling inside of her. She would have to be on her best behavior, at least until she got alone with Alex. She didn't care if her lack of control started a tornado; as long as she could be with him, she would risk it.

eighteen

By the time Alex arrived at the bar where Alma, Finn, and Dylan met with her friends, Alma had put down two strong drinks, her friends refusing to let her pay. Melissa and Carmen were both curious about the two men who had accompanied her, and Alma had struggled to maintain her composure, introducing the brothers as friends of her family. When Alex arrived, with Dolores in tow, Alma's status among her friends—as the luckiest woman in the world—was solidified. Alma could barely restrain herself as Alex approached where they sat on the patio, karaoke in progress. He wore a deep red shirt, matching her dress, with a fitted black blazer and pants. Dolores had worn a deep, dark green cocktail dress, which set off her creamy pale skin and vivid hair. Alma's friends hooted as Alex approached, immediately taking her in his arms and kissing her on the lips. "Happy early birthday, love," he murmured, smiling down at her. "If this was not such a frightfully public place, I'd be happy to take that dress off of you—as good as it looks on, it would look smashing on a floor." Alma felt herself blushing a deep crimson, her blood flowing faster from the combination of alcohol and steady lust. Even before Alex had arrived, Alma had found it difficult—in spite of the second potion Dylan had made her, stronger than the first—to restrain her desire-filled impulses.

Alex greeted her friends cordially before he noticed her drink was empty, and insisted gallantly on replacing it. Dolores settled next to Finn as Alma, deprived of Alex's distracting company, felt a familiar twinge of jealousy watching the two of them becoming very cozy. Her friends were vying for Dylan's attention in the absence of his brother's and Alma felt her impatience increasing the longer Alex was away. She looked around and saw him talking to the karaoke emcee, charming the woman with a ready smile, two drinks and two shots carefully cradled in his hands. He broke away from her quickly, making his way back to Alma.

"I'm sorry I was gone so long," he told her, looking directly into her eyes. "Will you ever forgive me?" Alma, slightly tipsy and feeling the effects of the increasing elemental energy flowing through her body, felt the push on her mind, the drawing in of Alex's will against hers. She raised an eyebrow, wanting to warn him she was wise to his game without saying anything in front of her friends.

"I will if one of those drinks is for me," she said, gesturing to the contents of his hands.

Alex grinned broadly and held out the two full cups, waiting until she chose one before he offered the shots as well. "Drink and shot, my dear. It's your birthday, after all."

Alma colored, taking one shot and downing it with Alex in the same moment. She chased the sharp, heady liquor with a sip of the refreshing drink he had chosen, for the moment indifferent that she was mixing alcohols. The alcohol entered her system and things softened, her sense of time deteriorating. It was fortunate she had Dylan to watch out for her, to make sure she didn't do or say anything she would regret. Finn, she thought when she wasn't drawn into Alex's warm charm, was useless as a bodyguard, wrapped up in Dolores's attentions.

It seemed like only a few moments later when the karaoke emcee called Alex's name, and Alma regarded him with shock.

"Didn't I mention? I love to perform," he murmured, giving her arm a quick squeeze that sent a jolt of intense desire through her. He gave her a little grin and nimbly trotted across the courtyard, jumping onto the stage and looking out over the gathered crowd. "I'd like to dedicate this to the most gorgeous birthday girl in the world," he said into the microphone, gesturing to Alma. She found herself moving closer to the stage, drawn as if a moth to a flame. He slipped off his jacket, and Alma was staring at him with unabashed lust, trying to control the rising wind that shuddered the leaves of the tree arched over the patio. In the span of a few heartbeats, she recognized the song: Muse, "Supermassive Black Hole." Alma's eyes widened and she thought her desire for Alex would either become unbearable, or squashed, depending on how he performed.

He had chosen his song well. Alma almost swooned as he sang, looking directly at her.

"Ooh, baby don't you know I suffer/ ooh baby can you hear me moan..."

His falsetto was nearly flawless, and as he moved into the chorus, Alma danced to the heady beat, not closing her eyes as the intoxicating sensation of Alex singing directly to her washed over her.

Alma inhaled sharply as the song continued, her hips shifting and twisting, her body swaying without direction from her brain, her instincts ruling her. She was smiling up at him, watching him move to the music as he sang, every moment calculated, she knew, to drive home his intense attraction.

"Glaciers melting in the dead of night, and a super star sucked into the supermassive...."

When the song ended, he bowed to the cheering crowd and leaped off the stage, immediately grabbing Alma and pulling her body against his, kissing her hungrily. The audience crowed their approval, but Alma was too lost in the moment, too wrapped up in the feeling of Alex's lips on hers, his tongue probing her mouth, his hands respectful but tight on her waist, trailing around to the small of her back.

Alma melted against him, willing to let the kiss go on forever, to let it intensify further. If Alex had begun stripping her free of the dress right then, she wouldn't have even cared enough to realize everyone was watching them. Power surged through her, freed of the suppressing influence of Dylan's magic and her grandmother's potion, fueled by the energy Alex was sending into her body through the kiss. She felt unreal—utterly disconnected from everything but the warmth of him, the taste of his lips, her need to feel him against her, to get rid of the clothes between them. She broke away from the kiss with a gasp, a sudden sensation like ice cold water showering over her, changing the intense heat of her desire into frigid fear. She felt a hand on her shoulder and pulled back from Alex, looking up into his intense blue eyes as her mind reeled from the abrupt change from amorousness. She glanced over her shoulder and saw

Dylan retreating, acting as if he had merely brushed against her as he tried to speak to the emcee. Alma realized he was the person who had touched her. He had managed to work a spell in a moment, jolting her free of the insidious influence of Alex's attraction. She swallowed against the sudden dryness of her throat and turned her attention back to Alex, who was looking down at her quizzically.

"Sorry," she murmured, leaning up onto the balls of her feet and kissing him briefly on the lips before breaking out of his embrace. "I suddenly remembered we were being watched." Alex stared at her a moment longer before nodding, submitting to her apparent change in pace.

It was not much longer before Alma had her turn. She gave the woman in charge a little grin, knowing she had chosen her song almost as well as Alex had—before he had made his choice, before he had even arrived. As the distinctive first notes of Fiona Apple's "Criminal" came through the speakers, she made eye contact with Alex, letting her voice drop down to a lower, more sultry part of her register as she sang.

"I've been a bad, bad girl/ I've been careless with a delicate man...."

Alma felt Alex's intense sexual attraction to her, couldn't take her gaze off of him as she worked her way through the song, tipsy enough to be relaxed but not sloppy. She forgot about every other person watching as she shifted her hips in time to the song; she wouldn't have noticed even an earthquake. She took a deep breath as the song moved into the climax, her body pulsing with vigorous energy, her nerves lit with lust.

"Let me know the way, before there's hell to pay/ give me room to lay the law and let me go/ I gotta make a play, to make my lover stay/ so what would an angel say, the devil wants to know...?"

There was a brief silence—no more than a few heartbeats—and the crowd cheered, almost deafening Alma as she stepped confidently from the stage and back into Alex's arms.

nineteen

She was barely aware of the rest of her party's turns on the stage; of Dolores singing "Super vixen" and Finn singing "Heart-Shaped Box." Both of them directing their songs at each other, and her other friends taking their positions and giggling through their more lighthearted songs. Alex drew her in more and more, and Alma knew that while self-preservation demanded she keep her distance and not reveal anything, Alex's subtle charms were working on her every moment. He kept her glass filled, kept her attention on him. She barely noticed the rise and fall of the wind as the evening wore on, and they moved as a group from the first club to another location, Alex keeping her hand firmly in his. The group decided against the strip club they had intended to visit, instead going straight to the preferred after-hours bar early, needing the relatively private atmosphere to decompress.

When the clock struck midnight, Alma was instantly aware of it; she was seated on Alex's lap, and before her friends could even sing "Happy Birthday," she was rocked with a power surge so intense she couldn't believe she had ever thought the ones she'd experienced before were potent. She reeled against Alex, who held her tightly, covering for the fact that she was suddenly overwhelmed. "You didn't tell me," he murmured against her ear. "I knew this was a special birthday—but you didn't tell me how special."

She knew he could feel the air energy rushing through her; Alma had never felt so intensely powerful in her entire life. She looked at Alex, smiling slowly. In an intellectual leap, a sudden connection of the dots of information she had gleaned, she knew he had intended to be present for her assumption of her full powers. He knew who she was; he knew she was nearing her complete transformation into an elemental. She kissed him briefly.

"Don't ever lie to me again," she murmured against his lips, knowing he would hear her despite the catcalls and hoots happening around them. "If you ever lie again about anything, I will make sure you lose the ability to lie permanently." Alex's eyes widened as she pulled back, her smile deepening. His hands on her waist tightened.

"My god, you're tremendous," he said, looking at her with actual respect in his eyes.

Alma nodded, the power inside of her making her giddy, giving her confidence she hadn't known she possessed. She knew with a certainty that if she had to kill Alex, if the situation demanded it, she could do it. She also understood, on a level she hadn't before, just how potent the powers involved in her elemental alignment could be. Her brain was filling with instinctive knowledge, her thoughts moving so quickly they ran together. At the same time, her lust reached a climax. She was filled with such desire that even knowing Alex had seduced her under a pretense didn't matter; she hadn't figured out his agenda, but she knew she would. But first, she had to get him alone. Her skin was crawling, her nerves shooting off impulses, her thoughts gradually centering on the need for satisfaction clawing at her.

Alma would never remember they had left the last bar of the night, much less how. She was consumed with the need to get Alex alone, to bring him to her bed. Nothing else would do; somehow, in spite of protests from Dylan, she was leading Alex up the stairs to her bedroom, closing and locking the door firmly behind her as the wind rose outside. She would have to be careful, she thought, in the part of her brain not consumed by lust. She didn't want to destroy the neighborhood. She was trembling, shaking from energy that was only increasing—she had to control it. She had to let it flow through her body. She had to put the energy to its proper use. Alex recovered from his shock at her sudden increase in power, and when she closed the door behind them, he pressed her up against it, kissing her hungrily, his hands wandering over her body in a way that was anything but respectful. He sought her zipper, pushing his body against hers firmly, anchoring her in the present even as her mind traveled a million miles away.

"You have to stay with me," he said, barely breaking away from her lips. "Stay here, in the moment. This is the most important time." Alma barely followed his words, too fascinated with his body.

She pulled his jacket off, casting it aside with no concern for its fine design. Alex found her zipper and tugged it, slipping his hands along the folds of fabric and slipping it off of her body. Alma stepped out of the satin puddle at her feet, letting Alex take her by the hand. He propelled her towards her bed, launching himself at her and pinning her to the mattress. Alma moaned as his lips connected with hers again and again, his hands traveling the curves of her body, sending electrical thrills along her nerves. She unbuttoned his dress shirt slowly, moving her mouth away from his lips and down his neck, kissing and nipping while her body arched and writhed as if it had a mind of its own, reacting to the momentum of Alex's caresses. He had her trapped underneath him, but Alma didn't care about her apparent subjection—she was too needy for his body, too full of desire to have any concern about which of them was on top. Alex guided her bra away from her body, tossing it to the floor and pressing his bare chest against hers while Alma worked the sleeves off of his arms, pushing his shirt away from him. He was lean, almost wiry, with sparse dark chest hair that brushed against her skin appealingly.

In moments, it seemed, Alma was naked save for her stockings, held up at her thighs.

"I quite like these," Alex told her with a charming smile, running his hands along the inside of her leg, the caress sending a chill of anticipation through her. The wind continued to howl, and Alma wrapped her legs around Alex's waist, pushing her hips against his, beyond ready to feel him. He chuckled at her impatience, kissing the tops of her breasts and working his way to her mouth. Alma was writhing, ready to use her powers—if necessary—to knock him over and take what she needed from him. Before she could make good on the impatient impulse, Alex was thrusting into her, his hips flush against hers, the friction building up between their bodies. Alma gasped as she felt the energy coursing through her body joined with Alex's power; she knew that she was sharing her sudden surge of power with him even as his powers were mingling with hers. She had to take control—she had to keep something back from him.

It was impossible to think as Alex picked up the pace gradually, touching her seemingly everywhere at once, murmuring into her ear as they moved together. Alma was breathless, inarticulate with rising arousal, her body taking over from her overloaded mind. Alex teased her relentlessly, picking up his pace and then slowing down, only to speed up once more, until Alma was crying out, panting for breath, strung out on desire. He knew exactly how to play her—as deftly as any musical instrument, drawing out the exact sounds he wanted her to make. Alma, even knowing she was being toyed with, couldn't marshal her abilities to fight him; she was too involved in her cresting lust to do more than ride the waves, to move her body in counterpoint to his attacks. Alex finally let her reach her climax, holding himself back throughout it, and Alma shook underneath him, shivering uncontrollably as pleasure rocked her. She held on to him tightly, struggling to catch her breath and realizing he was still ready for more—that he intended to wait for her to recover and then bring her to fever pitch again. With sudden insight, and sharp cunning that cut through the haze of her satisfied pleasure, she threw her weight up at him, knocking him from his position of power over her and onto her mattress. She tumbled him over onto his back, following him, pinning him to the bed.

"It's my birthday," she said, her voice hoarse and low with desire and the cries that had ripped through her throat. "I'm not going to let you call all the shots." She flexed her hips, smiling down at him.

Alma had complete control, pulling back her energy, drawing Alex's into her as she kissed him, moving on top of him, moaning against his lips. Alex was her willing prey, his hands moving over her body, trembling slightly from the force of his own pleasure. Alma smiled to herself as she brought him quickly to his own heights of pleasure, tormenting him as he had tortured her, bringing him to the brink and then pulling away, until he was growling and moaning helplessly underneath her, all thought of taking the advantage gone from him in the face of the pleasure she provided.

They took turns taking over control of their encounters, moving from the bed into the shower and back to the bed. Hours passing without either of them being cognizant. Alma felt the energy within her increasing more and more as dawn approached; it was the time of day most closely aligned with her element, and she knew when the sun rose, she would experience the final, thorough completion of her transformation. She wasn't sure whether or not she wanted Alex present for it, but her continual attraction to him, her constant need to renew the pleasure she had found before, made it impossible for her to send him away.

She reached orgasm underneath Alex for the final time as she felt it happen; she watched her limbs changing, glowing, even as orange-red light filtered into her windows through the curtains. Seized by the mixture of acute pleasure and almost painfully intense energy flow, her whole body convulsed against Alex's. The wind rose to such high speeds that Alma—in the part of her mind still capable of thought—feared for anyone in the area who might be outside. She realized despite the violent, consuming power coursing through her, she could have complete and utter control with only a tiny effort—a small exercise of her will. She pushed Alex away and clamped down on the energy, willing the wind to die down. She went into one exercise her grandmother had taught her, matching the wind to her breath, and inhaled and exhaled slowly, bringing the gale down to a steady breeze, attuning herself to it and letting it flow through her unimpeded.

When she came out of the semitrance, Alex was watching her, his eyes wide with recognition, fear lurking in the blue depths.

"Tell me the truth," she said, bringing her power of persuasion, her birthright, into sharp focus in her mind. "Tell me everything." She pushed out with her will, directing the focus of her entire mind on pushing past Alex's will. He fought her—his own abilities were not inconsiderable—but he was not as potent as she was. Words tumbled out of his mouth seemingly without his commanding them, rapidly, as if he couldn't explain fast enough.

"My family sent me after you. Dolores is seducing Finn to keep him out of the way; if we could have found someone for Dylan it would have been perfect. I was to seduce you, to win you over, to convince you to ally with us. We're all air elementals, and you are expected to be one of the strongest of our element in the world."

Alma sat up. She continued to stare at him as he spoke.

"I was to bind you to us with a betrothal, try to get you pregnant so you would have to depend on us. Once you were betrothed and pregnant, you couldn't get out of the family. You'd have to represent our interests with the elders—they would be your interests."

Alma's eyes widened. She knew the elders among the elemental community were important; they made decisions affecting everyone, they ruled on issues of whether a family could move up in the hierarchy, they even put severely compromised elementals to death if needed.

"Why the hell would you need me to represent you to the elders? Represent yourself!" Alma pushed herself away from Alex. She couldn't decide whether his motivations were better or worse for being somewhat personal.

"Your grandmother," he said. "She's—I can't tell you. I absolutely can't tell you. It was cast out of my mind, but it's her."

Alma shook her head. She had used the ability of compulsion on him; if he knew it, if he could say it, he would have.

In the next moment, Dylan came through the door. Alma felt herself on the verge of tears, though she wasn't sure why she should be so upset by a betrayal when she had known Alex had some ulterior motive. She didn't even care she was nude, that Dylan was seeing her naked, having obviously just had sex repeatedly with Alex. Dylan looked at her and then looked at Alex, who was still pinned down by Alma's compulsion.

"What did you find out?" Dylan asked her as the tears rolled down her cheeks.

"He was going to bind me to his family. They sent him after me, because they wanted to force me to represent them to the elders." Alma was appalled at the idea someone —even another air elemental—would manipulate her like that, would force her into a sort of slavery.

Dylan nodded, his face solemn, and he crossed the room, disregarding Alma as he recited a low chant. Alma was still reeling from the power that flowed through her, her thoughts assembling and breaking apart and reassembling in her mind. She glanced over at Dylan, who was standing over Alex, intensifying the spell he was casting, holding his hand over the other man's head. He finished, looking at Alma with solemn satisfaction. Alma watched as Alex fell into an instant, deep sleep, his body relaxing completely.

"We need to take care of Dolores too," Dylan told her.

Alma smelled the faint odor of smoke and heard unmistakable noise from the bedroom next to hers. She had a sudden, keen insight into her abilities, and she looked at Dylan with a small smile, climbing over Alex's helpless body and grabbing her robe. She slipped into it, unselfconscious in Dylan's presence, and the two of them went through her door and across the hall, opening the unlocked door to Finn's room.

"Do you trust me?" she asked Dylan lowly. The two in the bed were oblivious to their entrance, moving together in ecstasy. Dylan looked at her a moment before nodding. Alma took his hand. "Focus all of your water energy through me," she told him.

Dylan hesitated; a moment later, however, she felt the cold energy wash through her, not with the pressure of an ocean weighing down, but with the torrential quality of a gushing river. She pushed his energy through the air, focusing her intentions and murmuring a spell her grandmother had taught her but never explained. A storm swiftly assembled outside, and Alma brought the wind up, hearing it howl until the windows shook. She brought it on, more and more, reaching out and pulling together every ounce of magic she could. The windows above Finn's bed shattered and the storm poured through, drenching the intense smoldering heat charging between Dolores and Finn. The jolt of cold broke them apart, and Alma released Dylan's hand, focusing all of her will on the wind, pushing Dolores off of Finn, tumbling her off of the bed. "Now!"

Dylan repeated his spell, forcing Dolores into an instant deep sleep, suppressing her natural will. Finn launched himself out of his bed at Alma angrily, growling. She brought the wind around, deflecting him, throwing him back onto the bed. She made eye contact with him and held it. "Don't move." Finn's face flickered with confusion, and he strained against her will before subsiding, relaxing against the pillows. Alma's lust was cresting again and she noticed, that Finn was naked and still at the height of arousal, fire energy flickering through him, almost drawing her in. She gritted her teeth, keeping her attention focused on his face. Dylan finished his spell, stepped away from Dolores, and looked at his brother.

"You got the hang of that compulsion pretty quickly," Dylan observed to Alma.

She saw him smile from the corner of her eye. "Let me finish him." He strode to his brother and murmured a less intense version of the spell he had used on the two air elementals, saturating his brother with dampening water energy until Finn curled up on the bed, falling slowly into a light sleep.

"What did you do to the other two?" Alma asked, adrenaline working its way out of her system.

Dylan grinned at her. "A little quid pro quo. Alex will not stop dreaming about you for at least a month. Dolores, on the other hand, will suffer saddening dreams of loneliness."

Alma echoed his smile. "Sounds fair to me. Let's get them out of here."

twenty

Dylan sat alone on the balcony, savoring a beer by himself. Alma was in the deep sleep that accompanied the final awakening into her powers, her body learning to cope with the onslaught of energy while the power of air worked its way through every cell, finishing the transformation started in her childhood. He knew his own transformation was less than a year away, and he was both worried and unconcerned. It would not be as intense as Alma's, but it would test him. Finn was also asleep, no longer under the spell Dylan had placed on him, but exhausted, nonetheless. Dylan felt a grim satisfaction at the events of the morning; the final touch he had put on the two cousins who had successfully infiltrated Alma's life and almost achieved their goal of seducing her to their side had been a spell to obliterate the memories of their success. Dylan was thankful Alma's grandmother had taught him the spell—it certainly came in handy. The two meddling, manipulative cousins would know they had intended to subvert Finn and Alma, but they would not remember they had succeeded to a point.

Dylan's larger concern was what would happen next. Alma was in full possession of her abilities; the feats she had managed before succumbing to the deep sleep were more impressive than even Dylan had been prepared to see. He knew once she woke up—some twenty-four hours later—she would be even more powerful. Would she still need his and Finn's protection? He knew her grandmother's view on it: she would need it more than ever. He recognized what Lorene had said about her granddaughter. Alma was a potent elemental, but she was unstable. She had mastered her abilities in the moment, but the only way she would continue to do so—particularly the persuasion abilities she had developed so swiftly—would be for her to find a mate who could anchor her. One who was impervious, or nearly impervious, to her abilities. If she chose a mate who was less than stable, whose personality would bend to hers, she would quickly lose her grounding.

He had met one air elemental who had become compromised, who had lost control of his abilities and let them govern him, instead of the other way around. It was not a proposition that Dylan wanted Alma to face.

He needed to eat, and make sure he had enough for his brother. Alma wouldn't need food until the next day, and then she would be ravenous. Dylan decided his culinary skills were not quite up to the task—he ordered in. He was tired; not exhausted, but he had worked to the limits of his abilities, and he had reason to be proud of what he had done. He stood and finished his beer, walking into the apartment toward the kitchen. He would call Alma's grandmother later to apprise her of the situation. He considered that with Lorene's powers of intuition, she likely already knew. But he also understood she appreciated his calling her. Dylan had developed a rapport with the slightly prickly woman, founded on their mutual water-aligned characteristics and their concern for Alma.

There would be more work now, he knew; Alma would have to learn to control her newly powerful abilities. He looked forward to the trip back to her grandmother's house. Perhaps, if Lorene had time, she could help him further hone his own abilities. Dylan whistled to himself, moving around the kitchen, and thinking of how he and his brother could best ensure Alma's safety, knowing it would be a challenge.

what's next?

FLAME OF LOVE

Something is wrong.

Alma has come into her full powers but is more unstable than ever. Filled with dread, she visits her grandmother and learns her grandmother doesn't have long to live. Racing against time, Alma focuses on her training, absorbing all her grandmother teaches.

Before her grandmother dies, she transfers all her magic to Alma and warns her that *she* is now the key to war or peace in the Elementals world and she must choose a mate quickly--her safety depends on it!

When her grandmother dies, Alma turns to Finn for comfort, seducing him with magic, never expecting the fiery whirlwind that consumes her as their passion spirals out of control. With a heavy soul, she wishes she'd never used magic to compelled Finn to make love to her.

Has her reckless behavior destroyed any hope of a real relationship with Finn? He's sworn to protect her, but who's going to protect him…and her heart?

also by nikki riker

Nikki Riker

MILES BROTHERS ROMANCE

Hawke: Bad Boy Billionaire #1

Kade: Bad Boy Billionaire #2

Lars: Bad Boy Billionaire #3

SLEEPLESS SPADES MC

Cruz #1

Ryker #2

Kase #3

Calamity #4

www.ingramcontent.com/pod-product-compliance
Ingram Content Group UK Ltd.
Pitfield, Milton Keynes, MK11 3LW, UK
UKHW022235230426
12048UKWH00018BA/1269